LOVE UNEXPECTEDLY

A DOPE LOVE STORY

DAHLIA

SYNOPSIS

Veronica thought she had it all—a handsome husband and a life of comfort. The one thing her heart desired always eluded her. When her life is turned upside down by an unexpected betrayal, will she ever love again or find it in her to trust? When she meets dark, handsome Jay-D, he shows her a love that she's never experienced, until unexpected circumstances cause her to re-evaluate her relationship with him.

Jay-D is a man bent on revenge. His sole purpose is to make those responsible for his prison stint pay. Then comes Veronica, a woman like no other. Will his desire for her curb his plan for revenge, or will it fuel his reason to rid himself of past betrayals once and for all?

1

VERONICA

"Dinner has to be perfect," I anxiously said to my best friend, Trina. I was throwing a dinner party for my husband and the owners of his company, who I believed to be two idiots. I didn't know why I was so nervous. Every time we had a dinner at our home, it always went off perfectly, and I would receive compliments for days. Maybe it was because of the importance of this dinner, which was an attempt to save the company from filing bankruptcy.

"What's the worst that could happen? They won't like the food? We both know what you are capable of in the kitchen, honey. My girl can burn," she said all animated, and I laughed at her silliness.

"I know, I know. It's just this dinner is so important to Michael, and I want to make sure it's a success."

"Humph, that jackass," Trina said under her breath.

Trina had been my best friend since high school, and to say she hated the man I chose to marry was an understatement. They were always at odds and could never be around each other in the same room without being at each other's throats.

"Trina, that's still my husband, so not tonight, please," I said, sighing.

"Okay, okay, damn. I'm sorry. You just know how I feel when it comes to him," she sincerely expressed. I heard the alarm chime, alerting me someone had entered through the front door, which meant my husband had made it home.

"Hey. I gotta go finish getting ready. Michael's home," I said, attempting to end the call.

"Okay, and again, I'm sorry. Call me tomorrow to let me know how everything went, and I love you," Trina said.

"I love you too, crazy girl, and I'll call you tomorrow," I stated. Just as I was ending the call, the love of my life entered the room. Michael and I started dating my sophomore year in college and his senior year. He majored in business because he always said he wanted to leave behind a massive empire for his "heirs". I majored in culinary arts because of my love for food and my natural cooking abilities, which I inherited from my mother. Our relationship started off rocky due to his inability to be faithful and monogamous. After so much stress in our relationship, I chose me, and ended my relationship with Michael after continuous confrontations with his various women, and the one thing I couldn't excuse, an STD. Michael worked his ass off trying to win me back, and while it took us some time to get where we were, several years later, we were together and stronger than ever. The only issue plaguing us now was my inability to provide him with the heir he so desired, which led to the tension we were currently experiencing.

"Hey, honey," I said as this tall, chocolate god that was my husband walked toward me and pulled me into his strong, muscular arms for a hug and kiss.

"I'm sorry about this morning," he whispered in my ear. "I'm just so stressed about this merger."

"I know, and you don't have to apologize. I should have given you your space. It's just this last miscarriage has me wondering if I'll ever be a mother, and it just got to me this morning, and my emotions were all over the place."

You see, Michael and I have had several miscarriages in the past three years, and I was starting to feel as though my body was betraying me and that I would never have a child of my own. Michael stared at me with a blank expression and leaned over to touch my forehead with his as he proceeded to try to encourage me with his words.

"It will happen, but for tonight, let's get through this dinner party, and we'll discuss everything else tomorrow, okay?" I gave him a small smile and simply nodded my head, agreeing to his request. Once again, I suppressed my feelings and prepared myself to be the dutiful wife because, after all, that's what I was best at doing. He walked off to the bath-room in our huge master suite, and I heard the shower come on. I started gathering his clothes to put them in the hamper, and while doing so, I passed the mirror hanging on the wall in our bedroom. I stopped and stared at the woman looking back at me and wondered how our marriage had gotten to the point where simple conversations turned into huge arguments. I continued to drop his clothes in the hamper and got the whiff of a familiar fragrance but couldn't place it. I shrugged it off and continued downstairs to make sure everything was ready for our guests.

As I descended the stairs, the doorbell rang, and before our maid, Ms. Ann, could answer, I told her I'd get it. She turned around to head back into the kitchen as I pulled the door open. As I prepared to greet our guests, I was rendered speechless. Before me stood a man seen only in your most erotic dreams. He was about six feet three with smooth, dark chocolate skin, and a Morris Chestnut smile. I noticed a small dimple in his right cheek as he reached his hand out to me to introduce himself. I stood there staring at this chocolate god, until I heard my husband call my name as he descended the stairs.

"Baby, why do you have Jay-D standing in the door like that? Excuse her, man. She's been stressed all week, trying to get everything prepared for tonight," my husband said to his friend as he shook his hand and introduced us.

"Veronica, this is my boy Jayson, also known as Jay-D.

This man and I used to get in major trouble when we were growing up in Miami." I saw a hint of unexplainable darkness take over his eyes, and as quickly as it showed up, it was gone, making me wonder what it was about.

He smirked at me and licked his full lips as though he could read my mind and had just learned what was in my deepest thoughts. I softly said, "Nice to meet you," as I stretched my hand out to shake his.

He pulled me in for a hug instead, and as he pulled away, he looked into my eyes, winked, and said, "the pleasure is all mine." I grew flushed and hot all over at the look this gorgeous man was giving me.

As he followed my husband into the back of the house, I ran to the bathroom we had downstairs to gather my thoughts and prepare myself for what was going to be a long night. I exited the bathroom and entered the kitchen to make sure everything was ready for our guests. When I walked into the kitchen, I noticed the rest of our guests had arrived and were standing around chatting and getting acquainted with Jayson. He seemed as though he had the wives of the Damian brothers caught in a trance, and I couldn't help but laugh to myself because I was guilty of being enamored with him as well. As though he and I had some kind of strange connection, he looked up at me and gave me that dimpled smile that made me blush. I immediately busied myself because I had no idea what was happening between the two of us.

"There she is, the lady responsible for making this evening amazing, my beautiful wife." my husband announced to the room taking my attention away from Jay-D. He walked up to me and wrapped his arm around my waist and pulled me to him, planting a kiss on my left cheek.

"Good evening, everyone. Sorry for my delay, but if you all will follow me into the dining room, dinner is ready to be served." As I led the way into the dining room, I noticed my husband and Jayson exchange a strange look between them. I couldn't decipher the meaning behind it, so I shrugged it off as some special language they must have shared from their time growing up together. As we took our seats, the staff I hired for the evening served us dinner, and I started making small talk with Sherry, the wife of the oldest Damian brother, all while thinking I couldn't wait for this dinner to end.

2

MICHAEL

My wife didn't think I noticed the interaction between her and Jay-D. I'd check that shit later, but for now, I had to get through this dinner with these pompous assholes and Jay-D. You see, I'd been working for the Damian brothers for the past seven years, and due to their extracurricular activities, which included drugs, whores, and outside children, the company had been bleeding capital left and right. The only reason I continued to put up with them was because they had been friends with my father-in-law for years, and I had been trying to get him to hire me to work for his real estate firm for just as long.

Due to the popularity of his firm, he knew a lot of people, from politicians to movie stars and athletes. If you needed anything done in real estate in this area, he was the man to see. Hell, if he gave me a chance, I could take over and run the company, and he could retire and enjoy his money. But for now, or until my father-in-law came to his senses, I was forced to sit through dinner and suck up to Jay-D.

The tables had truly turned when it came to the two of us. I always had the aspiration to do and be more, and he used to be content being a part of the dope game, but that was years ago. It appeared as though he made some significant changes in his life, but from the way his ass was behaving with my wife, he never learned respect. I looked across the table at Ronnie, and she looked to be in her element, which was part of the reason why I married her, besides her father's many connections. Veronica was a real thoroughbred. Her father made sure when she was growing up, she had the best of everything. Designer clothes, the best schools, anything her heart desired, she had. Nothing was ever too much for his princess. I'd like to think that love was what got us here, but if I was being honest, my desire to make a name for myself and acquire wealth like her father, was what got us here.

I almost lost her at one point because, despite putting my ambitions first and needing her and her family connections, I was a young man with needs, and commitment frightened me. I continuously cheated and was sloppy with it, and not only did I get caught because of the women confronting her, but the STD I gave her almost ended us for good. I bust my ass to win her back and vowed to do anything to keep her. That was why I knew for a fact if she knew the real truth about her miscarriages, our marriage would be over. I'd been avoiding the question every time she brought it up. I wanted a baby about as bad as I wanted to live in filth and squalor on the streets, so it was important for me to steer her away from any topic regarding children.

I listened as everyone complimented her on her culinary skills and got a bright idea.

"Babe, all of these compliments you're receiving tonight makes me think you should start your own catering company."

"I agree," Sherry commented.

"I would definitely hire you; this food is to die for."

My wife gave me a puzzled look but quickly regained her composure and smiled at our guests, and replied, "It's something I considered, but we've decided to start a family, so I'm not sure if it's in the cards right now. But if I change my mind, I'll definitely give you a call," she said as she smiled and winked at Mrs. Damien. I chuckled at my wife who always had the right answer for every occasion. I slowly drank my wine and stared at her, realizing, at that moment, getting off this baby thing was going to be tougher than I'd thought.

As dinner came to a close, I had the men join me in my man cave for cigars and a drink while the ladies retreated to my wife's study to do whatever it was they did when we men weren't around. As the Damien brothers and Jay-D started discussing business, my phone rang, and I excused myself to take the call.

"Hello," I answered with an attitude after seeing the caller's name flash across my caller ID.

"Well damn, is that any way to speak to your son's mother?" Trina cackled into the phone. I immediately regretted answering her phone call, but I knew if I didn't answer, Trina would be on her petty bullshit, like popping up to the house with our son and making shady comments that thankfully always went over Ronnie's head, and I wasn't having that, not tonight of all nights.

"What do you want, Trina?" I whispered harshly as I clutched the phone with my fist wrapped around it so tightly you could see the white of my knuckles. "I don't have time for your bullshit tonight."

"You don't have complaints when I'm making you cum, now do you?" she asked in a nasty tone. I let out an exasperated sigh.

"Trina, what do you need? I'm currently in the middle of something, and I do not have time for your games."

"Oh yeah, your little dinner party you and the barren missus had tonight. I completely forgot," she said, letting out a sarcastic laugh.

"If you don't get to the point of this call, I'm hanging up this phone right now," I told her through gritted teeth.

"Our son needs some new shoes and clothes, and he wants to see your trifling ass tomorrow."

"See, this is why I didn't want any kids, let alone a child with you. I just gave you a thousand dollars last week to allegedly get clothes and shoes. What the fuck did you do with that money because I know it didn't go on my son!" I yelled, startling everyone in the room.

"You know what, mothafucka? You'll give me what I want, when I want, unless you want your precious Ronnie to find out about our son. Now, I expect five thousand dollars tomorrow and you to spend time with your son, or else, well, you know the drill."

Click!

I looked at the phone in disbelief because this bitch just hung up in my face.

"Ahhhh!" I screamed as I threw the phone across the room. I turned around to everyone staring at me like I had lost my damn mind.

"Excuse that outburst." I had to figure out a way to get rid of this bitch quick, before I lost everything.

This situation with Trina and myself started out innocent and wasn't meant to go this long. Hell, what we had was supposed to only be a summer fling. I was in college, having the time of my life, and I had no plans on settling down with anyone, let alone the campus thot. The best thing that Trina had to offer anyone was what was merged between her legs. She had absolutely nothing going for herself, so I was shocked when I realized she was not only roommates with but also best friends with the daughter of one of the most prominent men in our area. I made every excuse in the book to be at Trina's apartment when Ronnie was there, because my goal was to make Ronnie mine at any cost. The only problem I had with making that dream a reality was Trina. As soon as she felt as though I was more interested in Ronnie than her, she started threatening to tell her about our friends with benefits arrangement. I couldn't let that happen, so in order to keep her happy, I concocted a story about only wanting to be with Ronnie for her money and connections.

When I informed Trina of my plan to marry Ronnie and divorce her once I became established, she was all too eager to participate in helping me solidify a romantic relationship with Ronnie. The only problem was, there was a catch to our little arrangement. In order for her to help and not reveal my plan to Ronnie, we had to continue our situationship, which at this point, I was fed up with.

I never could understand how she constantly smiled in Ronnie's face and enjoyed the perks of being associated with her, yet she hated her at the same time. I'd tried to end the relationship numerous times, but things became complicated when she not only got pregnant with, but had my only son, and I harbored doubts about that as well. So until I could figure out a clean break, I had to keep her happy in order to maintain my current lifestyle.

"You alright, man? You seem like you're in LaLa land." I looked over at Jay-D, not realizing I had been quiet for so long.

"Yeah, I'm good. Just dealing with some bullshit, but I got it handled." *At least it will be handled soon*, I thought to myself.

"If you say so." He smirked, shaking his head.

I didn't know what his motive was, but his demeanor since I started dealing with him, as well as his interaction with my wife tonight had me questioning his motives. I knew our company needed his money right now, but if he thought he was coming into this situation and setting me up on some revenge type shit, he'd better think again. I would have his ass locked up as quickly as he appeared as a so-called savior, and this time, there would be no getting out.

3

JAY-D

I smiled to myself as I watched this stupid ass nigga talk to what I assumed was a bitch. This bitch ass nigga hadn't changed one bit. *He just got older and dumber, which is going to make my plan that much easier to carry out*, I thought to myself.

"You sure you're alright?" I asked as if I really gave a fuck.

"Yeah, just business," he replied with a smirk.

"Alright, business. You got that." I responded laughing.

The way he zoned out, I seriously doubt that was business. Michael thought we were cool, but his ass was the reason I did a five-year bid, and I wanted to make sure I tore his world apart and disrupted his life like he did mine. I remember it like it was yesterday.

We were returning home to Miami, after making a run from Texas, and got pulled over by the local sheriffs in the area. Now if we were around our way, the stop would have been no big deal, but we were pulled over in a redneck town where two black men driving a sixty-thousand-dollar car and wearing expensive clothes. That was what they would call a red flag. That redneck bastard took one look at us, and we knew what was about to happen. Michael looked at me and whispered, "Don't say nothing. I got this." They searched the car and found fifteen kilos of cocaine. We were arrested and taken down to the station where they tried everything in their bag of tricks to get me to talk, but I didn't give they asses shit. Little did I know, this bitch was over there singing like a fuckin canary. All they had to say to his bitch made ass was that they had been following our seller and that they had us on videotape, and this fool told everything.

I ended up doing only five years because of my age, but it wasn't even my shit. And the worst part was this fucka, who I did time for, took off and didn't help me with shit. I learned a valuable lesson throughout all of this though, and that lesson was that the only person I could depend on was me. I snapped out of my trance and asked Michael where the restroom was, because I was being suffocated by a bunch of pussy, and it wasn't the kind where it resulted in a happy ending, mainly for me. As I followed Michael's instruction on how to get to the restroom, I heard this laugh that made me stop in my tracks. I followed the sound and watched as this beautiful chocolate woman smiled and laughed and had everyone in the room captivated by her presence. Veronica seemed like the type of woman every man wanted to wife.

She had smooth chocolate skin, and her hair was in a natural wild afro. She was about five feet five, and as the old heads would say, thicker than a snicker. I must have really been deep in my thoughts because I didn't hear her approach me.

"Earth to Jayson," she said, waving her hand in my face.

I leaned over and whispered in her ear, "Unless you want me to pull your dress up and fuck you in front of these old ladies, I suggest you take a step back, because my man has a mind of his own." She looked down and noticed the slight bulge in my pants and gasped. I smirked when our eyes met and walked off to find my initial destination. Yes, I was going to fuck up Michael's world, and I might get a taste of Ms. Veronica while I was at it.

As I finished handling my business in the bathroom, my mind wandered to the things I would like to do to Veronica and the many positions I could place her in. I exited the bathroom and passed the kitchen with the hopes Veronica would still be in there, but while small hints of her perfume lingered, she did not. I found my way back to the den where I overheard the three stooges exchanging ideas of how to swindle me into investing into their company while maintaining control. Little did these bitches know, I bought the company from right up under they asses, and I was about to play the fuck out of homeboy. I cleared my throat as I entered the room and dapped Michael up, preparing to leave.

"Hey, man, thanks for the hospitality, but ya boy got moves to make."

As I turned to grab my jacket, this uncle Ben mothafucka jumped up yelling, "You can't leave. We haven't even gone over the proposal!" I looked this bitch up and down with a smirk on my face.

"Aye yo, playboy, if you want your face to remain on bags of rice around the country instead of milk cartons, I suggest yo' bitch ass refrain from telling a mufucka like me how to run his business, unc, feel me?" I asked as I sneered at him.

"I—I... wasn't trying to tell you how to run your business, Mr. Jay-D. I was trying to um, not waste your time is all," he stated.

"When I have my lawyers go over the proposal, only then will we discuss business, unc. Feel me? Until then, it's a no-go." I chucked the deuces and walked out the room.

As I entered the hallway that was off from the room I'd just exited, I heard her voice again and decided to get another glimpse before I left the house. As I entered the kitchen where Ms. Veronica was just ending a phone call, she looked at me and smiled.

"Hey, Jayson. Is there something you gentleman need?" she asked.

I walked up to her, and as I entered her personal space, I heard her breath catch as I whispered in her ear. "No one calls me Jayson but my moms and white boys in business suits."

She laughed softly and said, "Well I guess I'll be the only woman privileged enough, other than your mother, to call you by your given name." She grabbed a tray with coffee off the counter and winked at me as she walked off and disappeared into her study. I laughed to myself as I realized Ms. Veronica wasn't a prude like I thought. This was going to be very interesting.

4

VERONICA

As I stood at the kitchen sink, rinsing the dishes the ladies and I used, my mind wandered back to Mr. Jayson and our interaction tonight. Never once in my twenty-nine years had a man ever had my body reacting just from his mere presence, not even my husband.

"Do you hear me?" I jumped, startled by Michael's voice.

"I'm sorry, honey. I must still be tired from all of the cooking and planning. What did you say?"

"I said you and Jay-D seemed to hit it off rather nicely, huh? Did you not think I would notice that little interaction between the two of you in the foyer? My wife, the Prima Donna, acting like she wants to snatch her panties off and fuck a common street thug, right in my house. If only the great Tobias could see his princess now." He laughed nastily.

"I—I... don't know what you are talking about," I

responded. Michael got close to my face and stared me in my eyes with a look of pure hate.

"I'm glad you haven't mothered my children yet, since you feel it's okay to act like a common whore right in my face." He grabbed his keys from the counter and yelled over his shoulder at me, "Don't wait up. I don't know when I'll be back!" and slammed the door behind him. I slid down to the floor in front of the kitchen sink, wondering how we got to this place.

Michael had never been this nasty to me, let alone possibly staying away from home all night. I didn't feel tears falling down my face until I felt them hit my hands that covered my face. I slowly lifted myself from the floor, which was where I had been sitting since Michael walked out the door. I didn't know how long I had been sitting there or what time it was, but I needed to talk to someone. I grabbed the phone off the counter to call Trina, and she answered the phone right as I was about to hang up.

"Hello," she said, sounding out of breath.

"Hey, girl. Did I interrupt something?" I asked her, because I knew sometimes her son's father, who I had yet to meet, would come over to spend time with her and her son.

"No, girl. Hold on. Get up, bae," I heard her say to someone in the background. I heard shuffling in the background and then quiet.

"What's going on, girl? You sound upset," Trina asked me. I immediately broke down and told her everything that happened between Michael and me, and she was beyond pissed.

"I told you he's an asshole," she said, scolding me.

"I know, I know, but I love him, and I want our marriage to work, but I just don't know how to repair what's broken."

"Well it's not just your job to fix it. His ass has to meet you halfway, and if he's not prepared to do that, then maybe it's time for you to walk away," she said, sounding frustrated with me.

"Walking away is not always the answer to every problem, Trina. I just have to be more understanding. I know he's been under a lot of stress lately with his job, and I haven't been much help, constantly complaining about the miscarriages."

"Listen, it's your choice what you plan to do with your dead ass marriage and asshole husband, but don't expect me to always listen to you rant about a situation that you could easily walk away from. I mean, it's not like you need him for the money, Ronnie."

"You know what? It's clear you have your ass on your shoulder, and you've got some things to deal with, so I'll let you go deal with whatever it is you have going on with you."

"No, what you don't like is the truth, and I'm tired of being one of many, catering to the needs of Ronnie, like you're the only person with feelings and problems, so you know what? Call me when you have something else to talk about that doesn't involve your husband or lost babies."

Click!

Trina hung up on me, and I had no idea what had her so upset. My relationships with the two most important people to me was in shambles, and I had no idea how to fix it. Maybe tomorrow would bring better ideas.

I got ready for bed and lay down, preparing for a restless night's sleep, hoping for a better tomorrow.

The next day, I woke up to Michael's side of the bed empty and a ringing phone. I looked at the caller ID, and it was Trina. I rolled my eyes as I answered the phone with an attitude in my voice. "Hello, is this someone answering the ad for a new best friend?"

"First of all, bitch, I am one of a kind and irreplaceable, and if you even think about replacing me, it's going to be *The First 48* off in this bitch, except you and your new bestie's bodies won't be found." I laughed at this crazy girl and how silly she could be.

"Well you weren't being a good friend last night, so I figured I'd start putting out ads for a new bestie."

"I know, and I'm sorry. I was just in my feelings after dealing with my baby daddy, but I'm here now, so what do I need to do? Do I need to come over and bust the windows out that bastard's car, starting with that Masterati?" I burst out laughing at the way she pronounced Maserati.

"Um, no. That laugh you just gave me trying to say Maserati is enough for me." This was why I loved this girl. She made my darkest moments bearable, and I didn't know what I would do without her.

"How about lunch today, my treat, to make up for last night?"

"Sure. Just let me get up and start going. Where do you want to meet?"

"Our favorite place, The Cheesecake Factory," we said at the same time.

"Okay, is noon fine?" she asked me.

"That's fine," I responded. We hung up, and I started getting ready so I could meet my girl for lunch. One down and one to go, but I knew the second relationship wouldn't be so easy to repair. However, I was willing to put in the work. I was just hoping that he was as willing as I was.

5

TRINA

I lay on the bed, after hanging up with Veronica, and watched as Michael got dressed to leave me. All of a sudden, my heart rate increased, my hands got sweaty, and I felt a mix of hot and cold wash over my body. I was sitting there wondering how Michael and I had gotten to the point where he was married to someone else and I was just his baby mama. He was supposed to be mine, but just like every other man in my life, I became invisible to him once he met Veronica.

I thought I did things differently with him by not introducing him to her until I felt we were established. You see, Michael and I met the summer before I started my sophomore year of college. Ronnie had gone home to be with her family for the summer while I stayed behind to make up two classes I needed to graduate on time. I was walking across the quad when he came up to me with some fliers for a frat party that was going on that night. I was hesitant to go at first, but Michael could talk the panties off of a woman wearing a chastity belt—have her picking the lock and everything. Long story short, we ended up hanging out that night and the rest of the summer.

Once Veronica returned to school for the fall, things changed. He changed. He downplayed our relationship in front of Veronica, and when I confronted him about it, he laughed it off and said I was imagining things, but when they started hanging out without me, I confronted him again, and he explained his plan to get in good with her family to boost his career once he graduated. He used the lame excuse that he only loved me, and he was using her to build a better future for us. Several years later, and I was still the side chick, and she was now his wife.

"Why her?" I asked.

"What?" He turned around with his forehead scrunched up and his eyes slightly squinted as though he was both angered and annoyed at my audacity to question him.

"You heard me. Why her? Of all the women you could have married and fucked with, you had to choose my best friend, and I want to know, why her?" He rubbed his hand down his face and let out a loud sigh.

"Not this shit again, Trina. You know, I am really getting sick and tired of you asking the same fucking question when you already know the answer. Man, if you can't move on from this shit, then maybe I should move on from you." I let out this gut wrenching, rolling on the floor laugh that had Michael looking at me as though I had lost my damn mind.

"You see, you continue to play me as though you have the upper hand, like your precious Ronnie finding out about our son and what happened to her pregnancies wouldn't end not only your career but your life. What do you think Mr. Big Bad Tobias would do once he found out what you did to his precious daughter?" I asked, cocking my head to the side as we had a staring contest for what seemed like forever but only lasted for about thirty seconds. I turned around to get my clothes so I could take a shower, and Michael rushed me from behind, turning me around to face him and pushing me up against the wall by my throat.

"You bitch! If you tell my wife anything, I will end you, and we will raise Jamon as our own, erasing you from all parts of his memory, you common whore. You are nothing but a simple fuck, plain and simple, and if I even feel you breathed wrong in her presence, I will slit your fuckin throat, you hear me!" he screamed with spit flying out of his mouth and the vein in his throat popping out. I slowly nodded my head, and he let me go. I slid down the wall and sat on the floor as tears welled up in my eyes, and Michael stood over me breathing hard with his fists clenched.

"We're done. I will open an account for my son and make sure he has what he needs. I will stop by to see him, and if I even think another nigga is laying up in the shit I bought, I will end you. Now get yo' ass up and get ready before my son gets up." I smiled to myself because he knew he couldn't live without me. He didn't even want another man around me. We were not over, and we'd never be over.

He finished getting ready and left without saying another word, but he'd be back, and I'd be right here waiting on him so we could be one big happy family.

After I finished getting myself and my son ready, I checked myself in the mirror, and I knew I was that bitch. My hair was cut in a shoulder-length bob with the tips dyed blond, and I was wearing a pair of dark wash skinny jeans I got from Torrid, with a white halter top I found from Lane Bryant. I was a curvy girl, but I was thick in all the right places. My outfit stood out against my chocolate skin, and I was looking good, if I did say so myself. I threw on some makeup to cover up the slight bruises I had on my neck, and I threw on some silver accessories and a silver pair of Louis Vuitton sandals I bought the other day when I was at the mall, and I was ready to drop my son off to school and meet Ronnie for lunch. I just hoped I could control my emotions after the morning I had with Michael.

I ARRIVED at the restaurant after dropping Jamon off to school and stopping to get gas, and the parking lot was full, but I refused to use valet parking. Hell, I could use that money somewhere else. I scanned the parking lot to see if I could see Ronnie's car, and I didn't see it anywhere, so I figured she hadn't gotten here yet. I texted her to see if she made reservations, and she said she was already there, waiting on me. I went inside the restaurant to give the hostess my name but spotted Ronnie waving at me.

"There she is," I told the hostess and walked to the table where Ronnie was sitting. "Hey, girl. I didn't see your car in the parking lot. What, you plan on getting drunk so you caught an Uber?" I asked, laughing.

"Bitch, don't do me. I used a valet unlike your cheap ass, because I was not walking across the parking lot in this Florida heat."

"Well we can't all wake up and go to sleep next to a fine and wealthy man. I mean, we can't all be Ronnie Boudreaux!" I snapped.

"Is there something wrong, Trina? You've been snapping at me quite a bit lately. What's going on?"

"Girl, I'm sorry. It's just this baby father of mine has been such an ass to me lately. It has me lashing out at everything and everyone around me, so I need this lunch today."

"Well you know his godparents have your back, so you know he will not want for anything at all, so try not to stress too much, OK?"

"Yeah, I know. It's just hard at times." The waitress came to take our order, and I noticed Veronica ordered a water with her meal when she usually had a mimosa during brunch.

"Um, don't tell me you're not having a drink; today is not the day I need you sober." She started squealing and bouncing in her seat like she had to pee.

"What is wrong with you? Either you have to pee or something has you really excited, and being that you are old as hell, I'm going to go with the latter."

"Whatever," she said, slapping my arm and rolling her eyes.

"Now I'm not going to tell you." She poked her lips out and crossed her arms.

"OK, OK, I'm sorry. What is it?" A huge smile spread across her face.

"OK, so you know about the argument between me and Michael. Well, I was trying to figure out how to get back in good with him."

"Veronica, couples have issues. Nobody has the perfect marriage." I said, not really wanting to have another conversation about her and Michael's marriage.

"Are you going to interrupting me, or do you want to hear what I have to say?"

"Well excuse me. Continue."

"Well I got up this morning, and I just so happened to check the calendar, and guess what?"

"OK, I'm really not in the mood for guessing games, so can we get to the reveal?"

"Wow, you're a real bitch today, but not even you can spoil my mood. So anyway, today my period was supposed to come on, but—" she paused for what I assumed was for dramatic affect—"it didn't come. So you know what that means, right? I might be pregnant." My heart dropped. This man told me he made sure they were using protection and that she was also on birth control, and now here she was possibly carrying a whole ass baby, again. I was so sick of his lies and deceit. If he planned on leaving her why the fuck did he continue to get her pregnant, and then I had to responsible for ending the pregnancy. This shit is getting real old, and frankly I'm tired of his games.

"What do you mean you might be pregnant? I mean, I thought you all planned to stop trying for a while. You sure it's not stress? What does Michael say?" I was asking her a barrage of questions. She held her head to the side and scrunched her face in confusion.

"I thought you would be happy for me. You know this is something I've always wanted, so what is your problem?"

"Problem? Sweetheart, I have enough issues of my own, so what you have going on is the least of my worries. I mean, I just know your struggle, and I don't want you to get your hopes up to be let down is all I'm saying."

"Well I would hope that my so-called best friend would be happy for me and not acting as though I just told her I screwed her husband." I started laughing maniacally and shaking my head. It was like, in that moment, I realized my feelings for Michael was a game to him, and something in me snapped.

"Let me ask you something. You ever take a good look at my son? I mean really look at him and wonder who his father is?" She scrunched her face up and had a confused expression as though she was trying to figure out what I was trying to say. I shook my head and just looked at her.

"I tell you what. When you are lying in bed next to that amazing and perfect husband that you love to brag about, take a really good look at him and think of my son, and let me know what you think." I tossed back the last of my drink and got up from the table and walked away. I realized that I had some shit to figure out, and Mr. Michael was going to hear my mouth. I got to my car, and the first thing I did was call Michael.

"Are you fucking kidding me, Michael? A fucking baby!" I screamed into the phone as loudly as I could before he could even say hello.

"First of all, lower your gotdamn voice when you talk to me. Second of all, what the fuck are you talking about?" I pinched the bridge of my nose, and the tears started flowing before I could stop them.

"Unless you are fucking someone other than me and your wife, I'm not pregnant, so guess who in the fuck could be?" Even though this wasn't the first time this happened, and I knew he wasn't mine, the thought of him being with her didn't hurt any less.

"How could you, Michael?"

"First off, what I do and don't do with my wife is none of your fuckin' business, and second of all, I will take care of this one just like I did the other ones. One child I didn't want is enough for me. Now if you ever in your life call me on some bullshit about what goes on between me and my wife, a broken heart will be the least of your worries." He ended the call without so much as a goodbye, and I put my head down and cried from the pain I was feeling in my heart at this moment. I called my mother to see if she could pick my son up from school so that I could have a drink. My mother oftentimes wasn't the most reliable person, and Michael forbade me from having our son around her, but right now, I needed a break. I called my mom, and after what seemed like forever, she finally picked up the phone.

"Hey, Ma, you think you can pick up Jamon and keep him for the night? I got a lot of stuff going on, and I'm just not in a good place right now."

"Is it that woman's husband you keep messing with? You have always been the type to want what everyone else has instead of going out to get it on your own. I don't know where you get your trifling behavior from, 'cause it sure as hell ain't me."

"He was mine first, so why should I give him up? He doesn't love her anyway. He's just using her to get where he wants to be in his career, and then we will be one big happy family."

"You sound like a damn fool. *He's just using her,*" my mom said in a mousy voice, mocking me. "It's been several years, and he's still in the same spot. He's either dumb as fuck, or her father doesn't have the connections he thought. If I had a dollar for every time a man fed his side chick the 'I'm going to leave her when I get established' line, I'd be richer than Oprah. Grow up, Trina. That man has had plenty of time to leave his wife for you, and he hasn't yet. You go right ahead and wait around for a man who doesn't want you, and all you're going to end up with is a wet pussy and an empty bed. I'll go get my grandson. He needs to be around somebody with some sense anyway, and I'll call you tomorrow to come get him."

Click!

"Ugh, why does she have to be such a bitch," I said out loud to no one in particular. Everyone always had an opinion about me and Michael, but I didn't care. It was only a matter of time until we'd be together, and I wondered who would have the last laugh then. I pulled into a bar for a drink because I wasn't ready to go home to an empty house just yet. I walked into the bar Silk, which was an upscale tapas bar, to have a drink and a few appetizers. It was at the moment I realized I hadn't eaten anything because of my argument with Ronnie.

I glanced over the menu the waiter handed me and placed my order. I checked out the scenery around me and noticed a few couples in the building, and a wave of sadness rushed over me. I thought about all of the lonely nights and the missed moments Michael had when it came to our child and his milestones, and I realized that I was done waiting. I was done allowing Michael the power to make decisions with regards to our relationship. He was either going to make the choice to leave his wife willingly, or I would force his hand. Either way, he and I were going to be together because I was done with this waiting bullshit.

6

JAY-D

I sat at the booth in the corner, observing baby girl and her friend have a heated discussion. I was sitting here when she walked in, and she was so into her phone she didn't even notice me watching her. I got up as her friend was leaving and caught the tail end of their conversation. I walked up to her table and cleared my throat. She looked up at me, but it was like she was looking through me. From what I gathered from their conversation, ol' girl was trying to tell baby girl her son belonged to Michael, but it wasn't registering.

"Don't tell me you're one of those women?" I asked.

"Excuse me?"

I laughed at her squinted eyes and scrunched up face, which I guess was her attempt to look upset, but she just ended up looking sexy as hell to me.

"You heard me. Ya friend just low key told you she fuckin' your husband and her kid is his, and instead of cussin' her ass out, you sitting here looking all dumbfounded and shit as though you surprised it happened. So don't tell me you one of those women who so used to her lifestyle she can't let a nigga who doing her dirty go. Or better yet, you so worried about what people think, you stick it out just to not be the talk of the town. So tell me, which category you fall in?" I asked with my head cocked to the side, eyebrows raised, waiting for a response.

"First off, don't pretend to know who I am or what I would do as though you know me, and second, what goes on between me and my husband is none of your business."

"Well the way your girl just acted out, it became the restaurant's business, and trust me, I'm not concerned about you and your husband because you're not going to be his much longer. I'm just giving you time to come to terms with what we both already know and feel." I got up from the table and winked my eye at her and turned around to leave but was stopped by baby girl's voice.

"Jayson, Jay-D, or whatever the hell your name is. I don't know what you think is going to happen, but I love my husband, and whatever this is Trina told me, I can assure you there is more to the story, and he and I will work through it and come out stronger." I turned around and walked back to her table. I leaned over it to whisper in her ear, and I heard her breath catch. I chuckled at her reaction to me being in such close proximity to her.

"I know you don't believe shit you just said, and because of that, I'm not worried about anything. I always get what I want, and what I want is you, and the way you're holding your breath and squirming in your chair, I can tell the feeling is mutual." I leaned in so close to her ear, she shivered from the sensation of my breath touching it. I whispered, "Breathe." I walked away and left her sitting at the table without another word, but she knew this, whatever it was between us, was far from over. I hopped in my convertible to head north to my house on the beach. It was a place I went for peace and solitude, a place that allowed me to just clear my head and think. I knew this woman was making me care about her in ways that no other woman had. I barely knew her, and I couldn't understand the effect she was having on me. I realized I had to get rid of her dead weight she was carrying around with her, and that reminded me of my plan. I picked up my phone to call Michael.

"Hello?" He answered on the third ring. I jumped straight to the point because I had no time for pleasantries for his ass.

"Aye, when do y'all want to set up a meeting to talk numbers? I met with my accountant and lawyer, and they said everything looks to be on the straight and narrow, so let's meet. I have Wednesday free."

"Well it's short notice. I don't know if we can get everything together by then," he started, and I cut him off.

"My bad. You clearly thought I was asking, so let me correct myself. I have Wednesday available, and if you want this money, I suggest you make it happen. No wonder y'all bitch asses bleedin' money. Y'all don't know how to operate a fuckin' business. You don't want this money? If not, I can always put it elsewhere."

"No, no, we'll figure it out. I'll get with our attorneys to work out the numbers, and we'll talk Wednesday." I hung up without another word. I called my man Tech that handled business for me when I needed information on someone I was doing business with.

"Yo!" Tech answered the phone as usual.

"Aye, check this out. I need you to run a name for me. Veronica Boudreaux. Can you handle that?"

"Yeah. You want a deep dive or just the basic information?"

"I want everything, but can you get her cell number before we hang up?"

"Nigga, yo' game so weak you got to have your tech guy get a number for you? Damn. You need me to go out with you to give you a few pointers," Tech said, laughing.

"Bitch, the day I need pointers from your Poindexter, Steve Urkel looking ass is the day I need to hang up my player card. Now shoot me the number, with your bitch ass," I said, laughing at his silence.

"Fuck you, pretty boy. This Poindexter gets plenty of pussy. Hell, I might call yo' momma when I get off the phone with yo' bitch ass. Now check your phone. Peace." I heard my phone ding as Tech hung up. I looked at it, and it was a text with baby girl's contact information.

Tech was my boy. We went back to the playground, and he was always the smartest in our group of friends, always had his face in a book, but now he was using that smarts to run a Fortune 500 tech company that I was part owner in. He was my go-to when I was starting a new business venture, and if you had something to hide, there was no crevice you could place it in that Tech couldn't find. That's why I was glad he was on my side.

I stored baby girl's number in my phone as I was pulling onto my driveway and noticed a blue Mercedes parked on it and immediately got pissed. I blew out an exasperated breath before I got out the car. I watched as Leilani got out her car and leaned on it to wait for me. I took my time and slowly approached her, prepared to hear the bullshit I was sure she was about to spew.

Leilani was a beautiful woman on the outside. She had smooth, dark chocolate skin with thick natural hair that stopped just above her bra strap. She had full, thick lips I used to love to suck on while fucking her, and her body alone kept my dick hard when we were together. Leilani was what you would call a curvy girl, thick in all the right places. I had to have something to hold on to when I was deep in that pussy, and Leilani definitely had something to grip. The only problem was I found out I wasn't the only one gripping, so that was why I was trying to figure out why she had her ass here on my driveway.

"What are you doing here, Leilani? I thought I told you we were through, so I can't understand for the life of me why you keep showing up here." She walked up to me and wrapped one arm around me and allowed her other hand to grasp my man through my jeans. My body immediately reacted to her touch, which gave her confidence to go further.

"I missed you, and from what I can tell from your man, I'm not the only one doing the missing." I pushed her hand off me and removed her other arm from around my neck.

"You may let your pussy run you, but my dick doesn't think for me. Now keep showing up here unannounced and more than your feelings are going to get hurt, now leave," I said through clenched teeth. I walked off from her, and as I approached my front door, she started acting a damn fool. Leilani knew I didn't do that making a scene bullshit. I walked up on her so fast and grabbed her by her throat, she choked on her spit. I didn't know if my calm demeanor scared her or how quickly I jacked her up, but she got completely quiet.

"Whatever we had was gone, and if you don't get yo' ass in your car and leave, I am going to forget the love I had for you and show you the side of me you have never seen. Stay the fuck away from me and my home. Am I clear?" I growled in her ear.

She slowly nodded her head with tears running down her face, but that shit didn't move me in the least. I let her go and walked off, but before I could get in the house, she called my name.

"Jay!"

"What, Leilani?" I turned to look at her, and she just stood there.

"What the fuck do you want!" I shouted, startling her.

"I'm sorry. I just want us to get back to where we were. Is there anything I can do to make you forgive me?"

"If you have a time machine that can take us back to a time where you didn't cheat. Short of that, there is nothing you can do."

"I'm going to win you back, you'll see. Because no other woman is ever going to love you like I do."

"I hope she doesn't love me the way you did, Leilani, because I hope she loves me enough not to screw another man while supposedly loving me. Now goodbye before I forget I cared about you and get rid of you like I do my other problems." I walked into my home and left her standing outside looking like she had lost her best friend.

I heard a loud scream and crash. I ran to the front door and saw Leilani speeding out of my driveway like something was on fire. I looked over at my car, and she had thrown a huge rock from the landscape and broke my window.

"One of these days, I'm going to kill that bitch."

I called the insurance company, and they sent someone

out to fix it with no charge to me. Her ass was lucky, Geico just saved her life.

Once the guy finished fixing my windshield, I sat in my living room, watching TV, but I couldn't focus. My mind kept wandering back to Ronnie. I looked at the number Tech sent me and debated on whether or not I was going to use it. I finally said fuck it and took a chance. The phone rang four times, and just as I was about to hang up, her soft, sultry voice came through the speaker.

"That pussy still wet for me?" I asked her in my usual cocky tone.

"Who is this?" she asked, voice laced with confusion.

"If you have that many men calling you, then I need to get my gun ready for target practice." I chuckled.

"Wha... How did you get my number? You know this is borderline stalking and a little sad?"

"Well if I end up in jail for stalking charges, it's worth it for five minutes with you. I'm coming to get you tomorrow, so be prepared to take a ride with me, and don't have me waiting."

"I don't think my husband would like me spending time with a man that's not him, and I don't know you well enough to take a ride with you, Jayson."

"I love the way you say my name, but check this out, baby girl. Does it look like I give a fuck what your husband thinks? He could be sitting in the room with you and I still wouldn't care." I growled, getting pissed off at her attempts to put her sorry ass husband first.

"Well, Jayson, that's the difference between us. He's my husband, and I care."

"Then why are you on the phone with me? Is it because you're intrigued?"

The phone was silent. I looked down at my cell after what seemed like forever, and I realized she had hung up on me. I laughed because this woman was going to give me a run for my money, but I knew she would be worth the challenge. I opened up my messages and sent her a quick text.

Me: *Be prepared to bring an extra set of panties tomorrow because I'm not sure if I'll be able to control myself when I see you.*

Baby Girl: *You should be fine because I'm not going anywhere with you unless you're inviting me and my husband now have a good evening.*

I laughed to myself because Ms. Ronnie actually thought those words meant something to me, but I guess I had to show her I meant what I said. I always got what I want, and right now, she was at the top of my list of wants. I fixed myself a drink and relaxed my mind, thinking how everything I planned was falling into place, and before long, Michael's ass would be right where I wanted him.

7

VERONICA

After reading the texts that Jayson had sent me, my mind wandered to the events that had unfolded earlier that day. If Trina was telling me what I think she was telling me, then she and my husband had committed the ultimate betrayal. They not only slept together but fathered a child together. I replayed the conversation that Trina and I had at lunch and got pissed all over again. I was Angela Bassett lighting her husband's car on fire in *Waiting to Exhale* mad. If that bastard was near me now, I would probably kill him.

I thought of the losses and the years of heartache this man caused me due to his infidelities, and I wondered if he ever stopped fucking other women, or did he just get better at covering it up. I realized in that moment I was giving him something he could never give to me, and that was honesty, unconditional love, and loyalty. I checked my phone for possible missed calls or text messages from my husband, and there was nothing. It was seven o'clock, and I knew he wasn't still working because he was normally home by six, no later than six thirty.

I grabbed my keys and rushed out of the house, because my thoughts were driving me crazy, and I couldn't stay in this house alone a moment longer without answers. I drove around aimlessly for what seemed like forever until I arrived at my destination. I didn't know if I was prepared for what I was going to find out, but when I saw my husband's car parked in the driveway, I knew what Trina said at lunch was true. I attempted to calm myself down by taking deep breaths, but I knew it was no use. I got out of the car and slammed the car door with what felt like the strength of ten men. I banged on the door with all of my might, and when it was slung open by my husband, I felt my heart begin to race and a rush of heat all over my body as I took in the sight before me.

There were candles lit all over the place and two wine glasses on the coffee table in front of Trina as though I had just interrupted a romantic evening. Trina looked at me with a smirk on her face as she lifted the wine glass to her mouth to take a sip, and I must have blacked out, because the next thing I know, Michael had me backed up against the wall holding my hands with a tight grip over my head. There was blood coming from his lip, and my hand hurt like hell.

"You bastard!" I said, my chest heaving up and down. I was breathing so hard you would have thought I had just run a marathon.

"How could you? After all we've been through, you turn around and do this to me." The pain of my reality sank in, and I let out a gut-wrenching cry.

"Why!" I screamed, startling both Michael and Trina.

"Should I tell her or should you, Michael, since the cat is finally out of the bag?" Trina asked with a mouth full of blood. I tried to break free from Michael's grip and get to her again, but he had a death grip on my wrists.

"Bitch, we were sisters. How could you? Huh? Tell me was it worth it?"

Trina started clapping her hands together in a dramatic fashion like she had lost her damn mind, but I was about to be the one to help her find it.

"Don't give me that we were like sister's crap. We were sisters as long as I was willing to stay in your shadow, right!" she screamed, and her voice was laced with venom.

"I'm tired of playing second fiddle to the great Veronica Boudreaux, and for once, Trina Davis has one up on you." She looked over at Michael with a smirk on her face and slowly turned back to look at me with an evil grin while she asked Michael, "Should I tell her, baby, or would you like the honors?"

Michael turned around to look at Trina with sweat beads forming on his forehead and his breathing accelerated.

"Shut the fuck up, Trina," he said through clenched teeth with spit flying from his mouth.

"Naw, let her tell me. I mean, it can't be worse than you fucking my best friend behind my back, right, you bitch ass nigga," I said, mushing his head after I had gotten one hand free from his grip.

"Well," Trina started, "first off, he was mine way before he was yours, so let's get that clear now. He saw the Boudreaux name and knew the fame and notoriety he would receive from associating with your family would catapult his career to the next level. However, our man got greedy and had to marry the Boudreaux princess. The only problem is that he shared his little secret with me, so of course he had to keep me happy as well, soo, here we are." She drew out her last statement and waved her hands around for dramatic affect.

"And your son, Trina, is he Michael's?" I asked, already knowing the answer but needing confirmation.

"What do you think?" She cocked her head to the side with a smirk on her face.

"Let... me... go," I slowly said through gritted teeth. "I am done."

"Ronnie, let me explain." I slapped Michael so hard the entire room got silent. Michael touched his face then out of nowhere grabbed me by my throat and rushed me up against the wall with his body shaking from anger.

"If I don't put my hands on you, don't put your fucking hands on me," he said calmly, almost too calm.

He put me down, and I rubbed my throat where he had just grabbed me and had me up against the wall.

"Through infidelities, I have stood by your side. Once we made the decision to get married, this part of your life was supposed to be over. I lost my babies, and I felt alone through the whole process, and now I know why. What I couldn't give you, someone already had." I turned to walk out of the door before the flood of tears that were threatening to leave my eyes fell. I slowly walked down the driveway and almost doubled over from the pain that was plaguing my heart, but I refused to allow them the privilege of seeing me cry.

I made it to my car, and this sharp pain hit me in my lower abdomen. It felt like someone had stabbed me in my stomach with a sharp knife. I doubled over in pain, barely able to walk. I cried out because I knew what was happening. Once again, my body was betraying me, and I was losing another life. I reached in my back pocket to dial 9-1-1, and as soon as my finger dialed the last number, a pain hit me so hard, I could feel myself about to pass out. As everything faded to black, my mind wandered to all the recent pain I'd endured and what I could have possibly done to deserve it all.

I WOKE up to the sound of monitors and a blood pressure cuff wrapped around my arm. I frantically looked around at my surroundings. It took me a minute to get my bearings, but once I was fully awake, I realized I was at St. Mary's Hospital. I looked over and saw Michael sitting in the chair by my bed with his head in his hands.

"Get out," I said in a raspy voice due to the dryness in my throat. He got up and started walking toward me, and I put my hand up to stop him from getting any closer.

"Get out. I don't want to see or be near you right now, so just please leave," I said in a pleading voice. It cracked due to the emotional roller coaster I was currently experiencing.

"You need me here with you, Ronnie. You just lost our baby, and you don't need to be alone."

I started laughing, not because he said anything remotely funny. I was laughing at the sheer audacity of this man. He just revealed he was screwing my best friend and had a whole ass son that they both sat back and allowed me to be the godmother of, and he was sitting here pretending to be concerned about my well-being.

"Oh, now you're concerned? What the fuck do you know about my needs, huh? What has changed within the last few hours that you feel you know what I need or that you have to be concerned about me and my dead baby?" I asked, eyebrows raised with my head cocked to the side, waiting for an answer, but getting nothing from him but a deer trapped in headlights look.

"Just leave. I don't have the energy to deal with you right

now." I turned my back to him, letting him know I was done with the conversation. He stood there for a minute as though he was contemplating his next move. Eventually, I heard the door to my room open and close quietly. I broke down and cried for the baby I didn't have the real opportunity to get excited about. I was at a point where I did not know if I could go on or if I even wanted to go on after this.

The nurse came in to check my vital signs, and she tried to make small talk, but when I didn't reciprocate, she got the hint and left me alone. I once again turned onto my side and prepared for what I knew would be a restless sleep. I knew I had to make some tough decisions I wasn't really prepared for, but tonight, I was going to do what I could to rest.

I was awakened out of my sleep by the door to my room being opened. I heard heels clicking across the floor slowly, in what I figured was an attempt to be quiet. Who the fuck wore heels when they were trying to be quiet? All of a sudden, I smelled a familiar fragrance, and I immediately knew it was Trina. I continued to play sleep because I didn't want to talk to her, but I was curious as to why she was here to see me.

"Ronnie, are you awake?" I didn't say a word. I just continued to lay still and breathe as normally as I could so the heart monitor wouldn't go off.

"I don't know if you can hear me, but I'm not going to apologize, because he was mine first. You just don't understand the love I have for this man. I mean, I have his child for

God's sake. He never wanted a child with you. Hell, you saved us the trouble of having to make you miscarry because your body did it all on its own this time. Funny how things work themselves out, huh?" The more this bitch talked, the more I wanted to jump from this bed and beat her ass like I did at her house. People were always mistaking the bougie side of me for being unable to fight, but my dad made sure that I could take on any bitch that came my way.

I listened to this bitch spill her guts, and I felt no emotions for her, not a one, and if it wasn't for her son who I loved like my own, I would make sure she suffered a fate worse than death. Trina's time was coming though, and I would make sure she knew who was responsible for the misery coming her way.

"I want you to leave him alone, and I'm asking nicely this time, but the next time won't be so pleasant," she said, snapping me out of my thoughts. With her apparently feeling like she got what she needed off of her chest, I heard her feet clicking across the floor, and then the door shut. I lay in the bed with revenge on my mind, and the plan I had for both my trifling ass husband and friend would be epic. I couldn't wait to leave this hospital because the minute I get out of this place, they both would be targets for a revenge plot they wouldn't see coming. I drifted off to sleep with a smile on my face, feeling better than I had all day.

I WAS glad to be home after such a rough night at the hospital. I walked in the bedroom and started my shower, and I noticed the bed looked like it hadn't even been touched. My dad came in behind me with my bag.

"That sorry excuse for a husband should be here helping you. And he always wonders why I won't let his ass anywhere near my businesses. He can't even take care of home."

"Daddy, please don't start. I really don't have the energy to have this conversation again. Not today." One thing a lot of people didn't know about my father was that he was heavy in the dope game when he was younger. He got out when my mom got pregnant with me because he didn't want anything happening to his one and only child. He still had a leg in the game, which he thought I didn't know about. It was when he got angry that it showed, like now.

"I'm sorry, princess," he said, pulling me into a hug and kissing my forehead.

"Call me if you need anything else." Concern was etched all over his face.

"I will. I'm good for now. I'm just going to get a shower and try to get some rest. I'll call Michael if I need anything."

My dad looked like he wanted to protest and stay, but after a few minutes of contemplating, he reluctantly gave in and left, but not before reminding me that if I needed anything to not hesitate to call him or my mom. I got in the shower to wash the germs of the hospital off of me and to feel normal after a rough night. My cycle was still heavy, so I used my Lily cup, because for what I had planned for my husband and Trina, it would definitely come in handy. After getting dressed and comfortable, I grabbed my cell phone to call my husband to let him know I was home.

"Damien Brothers Agency, how may I help you?" the front desk clerk, Margie, said when she answered the phone.

"Hey, Margie, it's Veronica. Is Michael available?"

"Oh, hi, yes. I'll transfer you."

"Thank you," I told her. The phone rang about three times before his deep baritone came through the speaker, almost making me forget the recent pain he'd caused me.

"Michael Boudreaux."

"Hey," I said, voice laced with uncertainty and pain.

"Hey, how are you feeling? What time do you need me to pick you up?" He fired off questions so quickly I was unable to answer one before he was asking another.

"I'm home already. My dad picked me up." The phone was silent on his end because I knew he was wondering if I had told my dad what happened between us. I hadn't said anything to my father yet because he would kill Michael, and I wanted to make him suffer a little before my dad took over.

"Don't worry. I didn't say anything, but eventually, we will have to tell him because of your son."

"I know. I just need time, and we can tell him, hopefully, together."

"That would be fine, which reminds me why I was calling. I want to have dinner, just me, you, and Trina, so we can discuss how things are going to go moving forward."

"What do you mean how things are going to go moving forward? You're my wife, and she is my son's mother. I will spend time with my son, and that is the end of it, and Trina knows that," he said, raising his voice a little.

"I just want to be sure. So the three of us will have dinner say Friday?" I asked.

"Yeah, that's fine, and Ronnie, I'm sorry, and I still love you."

"I know. Just make sure to extend the invite to Trina. I don't feel like speaking to her right now. I'll be cordial because of your son, but she gets nothing else from me."

"OK, I understand, and I'll make the phone call," Michael said, sounding defeated.

I hung up the phone and lay down to get some rest. My plan was going just how I expected it to.

8

MICHAEL

I hung up the phone with Veronica feeling so dejected. I could hear the hurt and pain in her voice, and it really hurt me to my core, realizing that I was the one responsible for the pain she was feeling. The fact that there was a possibility that I could lose her, had me realizing how much I really did love this woman, and I would do anything to keep her. Our relationship initially began as a way for me to come up, but I now realized that, at some point, I really fell in love with her. I was not losing her for anyone, Trina included. I let out a long sigh as I ran my hand down my head and face. I looked up, and Jay-D was just walking into my office.

"Damn, nigga. You look stressed. What's going on with you?" he asked, sitting in the chair across from my desk.

"Just some personal things going on at home, but nothing I can't handle. You ready for this meeting? Everyone should be waiting on us in the conference room," I said, standing up so I could lead the way to the meeting. Jay-D stood up to follow me into the conference room. As we walked in, all eyes were on us.

"Good afternoon, gentlemen. I guess we can get started since everyone is here," one of the Damian brothers said as we took our seats at the table.

"Well I wouldn't say everyone's here. I'm still waiting on a couple of the members from my team, so how about we go around the table introducing ourselves until they get here." The shorter and ugliest of the Damien brothers sucked his teeth and looked at Jay-D like he wanted to say something, but he thought twice when Jay-D stared at him as though he was begging him to disagree so he could set him straight. By the time everyone got done introducing themselves, Jay-D's team was walking into the conference room, and he looked at the Damian brothers with a smirk and confidence that I couldn't make out.

"We can get started now," Jay-D said to the group at the table.

"Aren't they going to introduce themselves like everyone else did?" the taller of the Damian brothers asked. Jay-D pinched the bridge of his nose with his head down and let out an exasperated sigh like he was a question away from letting the Damian brothers have a piece of his mind.

"If you needed to know who they were, you would. Now let's get started," he said through gritted teeth. While they went over the numbers, I couldn't believe how far in the red these two fools had gotten us. If looks could kill, Carl and Charles would be dead on sight, because all of us sitting at the table had death stares directed straight at them.

"What the fuck is this shit, Carl and Charles? We appear to be one deal away from losing everything, so tell me what the plan is, 'cause y'all fuckin' with my money, and this here is some bullshit," I said, standing up, balling the paper up and tossing it in their direction.

"I want to know what you two were thinking 'cause it's clear y'all didn't think we'd find out, so what now?"

Charles stood up, looking at all of us with a grimace on his face and huffing and puffing like a dog who had been left out in the sun.

"These are all lies," he said, tossing the folder Jay-D gave him with all the information he collected, across the table. He pointed his fingers at Jay-D and his team as he continued to rant and rave.

"I don't know what you are trying to do, but my brother and I have run a reputable company for thirty years, and we will not allow some felonious thug to come in and take everything we worked for out from under us. Now you and your people can get the hell out of my building, and we'll look for another investor," he said, plopping back down in his chair.

Jay-D let out a sinister laugh, one where he sounded as though he was one snap away from a straitjacket. I looked over at him, and as quickly as the laugh started, it ended. I had never seen the look Jay-D had on his face on anyone. His eyes looked cold and lifeless like he could kill someone with just a look, and just as quick as the look flashed across his face, it was gone. What I knew at that moment and what the Damien brothers were definitely not privy to, was that the brothers were playing with fire, and messing with Jay-D and his money, they were definitely about to get burned. Jay-D leaned across the table and looked at them until they both started fidgeting in their seats.

"I think there has been a miscommunication with regards to why this meeting was called. I'm not interested in investing in your company because I already purchased it out from under you. See, there were some very unhappy investors that held stock in your company, and they weren't pleased with the way you two handled your business. I made all of them an offer they couldn't refuse, and they didn't resist, so what was it you said a few minutes ago? Oh yeah, get the fuck out of my building." Two big dudes with security jackets came in to escort the Damien brothers out of the building, and they were screaming obscenities and threats of a lawsuit, but Jay-D looked completely unfazed and unbothered by their antics.

He looked at all of us, and me in particular when he started discussing an audit of each of our expenditures at the company and said he would be meeting with each of us one on one in the coming weeks. The meeting ended, and I went back to my office, scared as fuck. I was stressing because I knew there were a few times I used the company card to purchase things for Trina and my son so that Ronnie wouldn't find out.

"Fuck, fuck, fuck," I said out loud. I didn't know how the fuck I was going to get out of this. If it was a couple hundred dollars here and there, it would be no big deal, but I put a down payment on a car, gave her money off that card, and God knows what else. I always paid it back, but it just didn't look good using a company card for personal reasons. The Damian brothers let me slide with a whole lot of shit, but Jay-D seemed like a stickler for his business, and I knew he was not about to let shit slide. I called my secretary and told her to pull all the credit card statements and receipts for my business card and shred them, trying to buy myself some time. I knew he would have to have things switched over, so he might not have immediate access to the accounts. Therefore, I might be good for a while, or at least until I found a solution to my problem. I let Carla, my personal secretary, know I was leaving for the day and to reschedule all of my meetings.

I left the office and headed to Trina's house, because something had been plaguing me since the night Ronnie lost the baby. She had never popped up to Trina's house without calling first, and something made her come over that night, and I wanted to get down to the bottom of it. I pulled up onto Trina's driveway and parked behind her car. For this bitch to have a job, she was always home. No wonder she always stayed in my pockets.

Ronnie finding out about my son was making me see Trina in a whole new light, and it wasn't good. I opened the door with my key, and she wasn't in the living room. I checked the kitchen and the backyard and nothing. I noticed the house was filthy though. Trina never kept the house like this. She always kept the house clean, but of course, she always knew when I was coming. There were dishes piled up in the sink with caked on food, the garbage smelled like it hadn't been taken out in days, and the den had clothes on the couch and all over the floor. It made me wonder was she always like this or was it because of everything that went down. I entered her bedroom and it was dark, the blinds were closed, and she had the blackout curtains closed, making it look like it was night out instead of two o'clock in the afternoon. I could make out her silhouette on the bed, but she didn't make a move to get up or to even acknowledge I had even walked in the room. I turned the light on, and she sat up in the bed looking like she hadn't changed clothes or taken a bath since I left for the hospital with Ronnie.

"What the fuck is wrong with you, and where is my son?" I looked around, realizing he wasn't home from school yet.

"Why the fuck do you care? You haven't called or been by to see him since your little wife had her incident, so don't pretend to care now." She laid back down in the bed, pulling the covers over her head. She was talking to me with her back turned to me, and it was pissing me off. I walked around to the other side of the bed so she would be facing me, and I snatched the covers off of her, and the smell that was coming from her almost made me vomit.

"When was the last time you got your ass up to bathe? You fucking smell like ass and hot garbage. Get your ass up, take a shower, and meet me in the living room." I grabbed her cheeks, squeezing them. "And don't have me waiting, or the next stench coming from you will be your rotting corpse, now move." I walked out the room as she sat up in the bed sighing and mumbling under her breath but moving to get a shower. I headed toward the den to wait for her to finish, and while I was waiting, I started cleaning up the garbage that she had spread all over the kitchen. By the time I finished taking the garbage out, she was coming down the hallway into the den where I was sitting. She came out with no makeup, her hair in a ponytail, and a t-shirt and sweats on. Trina has always been a beautiful woman; it was just her attitude that made her severely unattractive. I looked at her, shaking my head, wondering how this conversation we were about to have was going to turn out.

"So you want to explain to me why this house looks like a ratchet ass hood rat lives here, with shit all over the place like you living in the gotdamn projects?" I sat staring at her, waiting for a response, and got no answer.

"Trina, we have a son to raise, and you can't be lying around here moping like a fucking child because I choose to put my wife first. Are you really that fucking stupid?" I asked her with my eyebrows scrunched up in frustration. Trina looked at me with so much pain and anger in her eyes that it caught me off guard when she reared back and slapped me. I swear it felt like my teeth shook. I counted to ten in my head before reacting because I know she was hurt, but there wouldn't be too many more of those slaps. I looked at her with eyes squinted and jaw clenched, and I spoke to her calmly and slowly but serious enough that I got my point across.

"I don't put my hands on you, and unless you want that to change, I suggest you keep your fucking hands to yourself."

"You lied to me all this time, and you think that you are going to be able to ride off into the sunset and live happily ever after with the next bitch? I don't think so. It's me and you in this here situation, and no matter how much guilt you feel, that is not going to change. Besides, after the little visit I had with the wifey, I doubt very strongly that your wife will want the fairytale ending, at least not with you anyway." She looked at me with a sinister smirk and a self-gratifying look on her face.

"What the fuck do you mean by that? And when did you go see my wife?"

The comment Trina made had me nervous about going home because I knew whatever she told her couldn't be good for my marriage. I stared at her, waiting for an answer, and she continued to look at me like she was hiding a secret only she had the answer to, and she had no plans on telling me. She slowly rose from the couch and leaned toward me just close enough to where if she puckered her lips, she would kiss me.

"You and me," she said, pointing at both of us simultaneously, "will never be over, no matter how hard you try and how much she wants you to herself. The quicker you and her get used to the idea, the quicker we can all move on. Now what would you like for dinner?" She looked at me and smiled. I swear her moods were switching so fast. I was scared as hell and had to get out of here as fast as I could.

"I promised Ronnie I would be home for dinner." I lied. "But raincheck?" I asked her. At first, she squinted her eyes in anger but smiled at the same time, which let me know this bitch was crazy and I needed to get the fuck out of here. I rushed out of the house without saying goodbye, and I got in my car and headed home. I called my wife to feel her out before I got home.

"Hello," she said, sounding happy, which eased my mind a little because whatever Trina said couldn't have been that bad.

"Hey, how are you feeling? I'm sorry I was unable to pick you up when you got discharged. I need to call your dad and thank him," I said, meaning every word.

"I'm good. A little wave of sadness washes over me from time to time, but I'm good. What about you? How does it feel to be married to a broken woman?" she asked me with a hint of sadness in her voice.

"You're not broken. It just isn't our time to have a child yet, but when it's time, we will have the picket fence, the dog and 2.4 kids," I said to her, trying to lighten the mood. She sighed a little but agreed to what I was saying.

"Well you already got a head start." She mumbled, but I pretended not to hear.

"Do you need me to pick up anything while I'm out?"

"No. I'll just see you when you get here."

"I love you," I said to her, but she had already hung up the phone. I turned the music up and braced myself for the blowback from the argument with Trina and the revelation that she had a conversation with my wife without my knowledge. I was not ready for the consequences from any of this, but I did know I would do anything to keep my wife from leaving, including giving her the baby she wanted.

9

JAY-D

I sat at my desk, reviewing paperwork, when I heard a knock on my door.

"Come in," I answered, and the receptionist, Margie, walked through the door with a stack of papers in her hand.

"Here are the papers you asked me for, Mr. Thomas," she said to me as she handed me the papers that Michael asked her to shred. I laughed at how stupid this fool was. You're going to shred papers immediately after a meeting discussing an audit of each employee with access to expenditure accounts. I shook my head and laughed because that fool was making this too easy.

"Thanks, Margie. That will be all." Margie exited my office, and I continued to look over the paperwork she handed me. I noticed Michael had been making huge purchases and paying them off himself, but recently, he was spending but not covering his expenses. I also noticed Margie had added recent expenditures for the Damian brothers, and I noticed a lot of money was coming in, but no new accounts were being acquired. This had me wondering how the Damian brothers really made their money and what kind of shit they had their hands in, because I knew there was no way they could possibly be staying afloat with the accounts they currently had. I reached out to my boy Tech and had him do a deeper dive into the Damians' accounts to see what they weren't reporting. I told him to also see what else Michael was linked to when it came to the Damians', and to hit me up once he had an answer. I turned my chair to the window, which gave me a beautiful view of the ocean. My mind wandered to the short conversation with Ronnie, and I found myself dialing her number.

"Hello." Her soft, sultry voice came through the speaker on my phone.

"You ready to take that ride with me?" I asked her, knowing that she wasn't going to answer my question.

"Once again, I ask you, if you're asking for me and my husband to take a ride with you, then of course we're in, but if it's just me you're asking for, then I have to pass. I'm not that type of woman. And where would *we* be going if we chose to say yes?" she asked, putting emphasis on the word 'we', trying to be a smart ass. I called her bluff while letting her know she was setting herself up to have problems with her husband if that was how she wanted to handle things.

"You can invite him when I pick you up in a few, but be forewarned. That won't change how I act when I'm with you, so if you want to fuck up your marriage, then by all means, bring him along." Her side of the phone got quiet, and I knew she was mulling over what I had just said to her and contemplating on whether or not she should take her chances and invite him along with us.

"Look, just come take a ride with me. I promise to be on my best behavior, and from the sound of your voice, you sound like you could use a friend, even if it's just to be quiet and listen. I'm fifteen minutes away, so be ready when I get there." I hung up the phone, not even waiting for a response from her because I knew if I gave her an option of whether or not to go with me, she would surely back out. I shut down my computer and locked the papers Margie gave me in my safe before locking up my office and leaving. I hopped in my car and headed in the direction of baby girl's home, and because the traffic was light, I got there in under fifteen minutes. She must have been watching out for my car, because as soon as I pulled up, she was walking out the front door.

She stood at the top of the steps with her arms crossed and a slight scowl on her face. Her attempt at looking angry made me smile because no matter how mean she tried to look, her beauty made it impossible for me to take her anger seriously. I got out of my car and walked around to the passenger side and leaned against the door, looking up at her without a smile, which I knew was making her uncomfortable by the way she kept shifting her weight from foot to foot.

"What did I tell you over the phone, Jayson?" I had to adjust myself, because the way she said my name always took my mind to thoughts of what I would do to her once she was mine.

"Do you hear me, Jayson?" she asked, sounding irritated with me because I clearly wasn't listening or paying attention to what she was saying. Anything she said that didn't include her getting in my car was irrelevant.

"No, because my mind was on how many ways I can make you cum while you call my name," I said without a smile gracing my face. I walked up the steps slowly, never taking my eyes off of her, making her even more uncomfortable than she already was.

"I'm not a man who is used to asking a question more than once, so I suggest you take heed to my request, or you are going to find yourself thrown across my shoulder and being placed in my car against your will. I would prefer for you to come willingly, but I'm not above forcing you to come with me. I mean that literally and figuratively," I said, looking directly in her eyes without blinking. We stood there for what seemed like forever, in a staring match and a battle of wills, until she came to her senses and walked around me and got in the car, slamming the door in the process. I stood outside her door, staring at her through the window before walking around to the driver's side and getting in the car. I sat for a minute watching her sulk before pressing the button to start my car. I leaned over the armrest and got so close to her I heard her breath catch.

"I don't care how fine your ass is. The next time you slam my car door, I'm going to give you something to tame that attitude," I said, kissing the side of her face and pulling off, letting the windows down and turning the music up.

"Well since you are holding me against my will, the least you can do is tell me where we're going, Jayson," she said, turning my music down, thinking I was going to answer her question.

I ignored her for a brief second before I smiled and turned the music up, telling her to just enjoy the ride. We rode about an hour north of Palm Beach and ended up at a restaurant near the water called 2nd Street Bistro in Fort Pierce. We got lucky as we pulled up to the restaurant because there was someone pulling out of a parking spot that was on the street directly in front of it. I got out of the car and walked around to the passenger side of the car to open Ronnie's door for her. She sat for a minute before she reluctantly got out and walked to the front door, leaving me at the car alone to lock up. I stood behind her in the restaurant and wrapped my arms around her waist and leaned over her shoulder and whispered in her ear.

"This isn't going to go well tonight if you continue to fight me. Let go for one night, and I promise you it will be magical." I stood up and winked my eye at her and asked the hostess for a table on the patio since there was such a nice breeze coming in off the water. She followed behind me, and when we sat down at the table, I noticed a shift in her demeanor. The waitress handed us our menus, and we sat in silence, contemplating what we wanted. When the waitress returned, I gave her my order, and baby girl did the same. We sat in silence for so long the waitress was returning with our food. She looked so peaceful that I didn't want to disturb her. She looked down at the food.

"This looks good. I can't wait to try it."

"If you think this is good, wait until you've had the Finger Lickin wings from Phatz. It will change your life," I said with a chuckle.

"I bet," she said with a smile. After she had taken a few bites of her food, she started talking, and I just listened.

"I'm sorry for how I've been acting tonight. I've just had a lot going on, and it has nothing to do with you, so I shouldn't take out my frustrations on you. Can we start over?" she asked me so softly I almost didn't hear her.

"It's all good," I said to her.

"You want to talk about what's going on? Maybe an outside party can give you some clarity."

She let out a soft chuckle and looked at me with the saddest eyes, and I just wanted to protect her from the pain she was experiencing at this moment.

"Thank you, but it's some stuff I have to figure out on my own. So tell me a little about you. How long have you known my husband, and how is it that a man that calls himself my husband's friend, continues to go after his wife? You can't like him very much, so what's that about?" she asked with an innocent expression on her face.

It was my turn to chuckle because baby girl didn't miss a beat and was a straight shooter which I liked.

"Your husband and I met years ago, and something happened where we lost contact, and I didn't get the opportunity to show him the gratitude he so deserves, so that's kind of why I felt this business opportunity was the perfect chance to show him my eternal gratitude," I said as I sipped my drink and stared at her at the same time.

"Well that sounds a bit sinister to me." Her face scrunched up and skepticism was in her voice. I chuckled at her ability to pick up on subtle clues.

"I'll just say he'll never forget what friendship means in the end. But enough about him. Are you ready to get out of here, because you seem to be done eating?" I asked, hoping she wasn't ready to end the night because the conversation between us was simple, easy, and if I was being honest, I wasn't ready to take her home.

"Yes. I think I've been gone long enough, and I left my phone home, so I know my husband is probably wondering where I am."

"Who said I was taking you home? Let his bitch ass

wonder for one night. Let's go." I got up from the table and threw enough money on it to cover the bill, as well as a hefty tip for the waitress, before I pulled her chair out so she could get up and we could head out.

"We're not far from the water. Let's take a walk over and sit for a few." I grabbed her hand as we headed over to the waterway near the downtown library. The area was nice and quiet with people fishing from the boardwalk and families and lovers enjoying the saltwater breeze that only people living near the ocean got to experience. I grabbed her hand as we walked in silence, and to my surprise, she didn't pull away. We sat on one of the many benches that lined the sidewalk in front of the waterway and just enjoyed each other's company.

"Why me?" she asked out of the blue, eyebrows raised and signs of confusion all over her beautiful face.

"I'm a married woman with a lifetime worth of baggage that comes with me, so what is your angle, and don't lie to me and say nothing, because that would insult both of our intelligence." I let out a soft chuckle before looking her directly in her eyes and answering her question.

"Why not you? You think I give a fuck about a wedding ring? In case you haven't figured me out yet, let me let you in on a little secret. When I want something, I go after it until it belongs to me, and I want you. I've wanted you since the first time I laid eyes on you at your dinner party. Your husband is just an obstacle that won't be in my way much longer."

"What is that supposed to mean?" she asked, snapping at me. I stood up and started walking toward my car to avoid a scene. She followed suit, still questioning the meaning behind my statement. When we almost got to my car, I turned around and did something I had been wanting to do all night, and that was kiss her. At first, she was returning the gesture and let out a slight moan. When I tried to pull her in closer, she snapped out of it and pushed away from me, breathing heavily.

"Why did you do that?" she asked, sounding as though she was attempting to catch her breath after almost drowning. I smiled and walked closer to her and leaned over and got as close to her ear as I could and said, "You're mine, and don't forget it. Now get in so we can go."

She got in without an argument, and I smirked at the way her face was balled up, trying to make sense of everything that was happening tonight. As we got on 95 headed back to her house, we rode in complete silence, listening to "Losing" by H.E.R, which I purposely played.

My ambition is attractive
My aggression isn't passive
I promise with you the butterflies in my stomach are active
They're dancin', I'm feelin' static
Wanna get closer like magnets
Your company, I've been feinin'
I think I've turned to an addict I don't get high
But lookin' in your eyes, I'm lifted

Can we make this tradition?

Your kisses make all my doubts go away

Go away, yeah

H.E.R.'s music was like poetry. She could put how you felt in words. Baby girl stared out the window and listened to the lyrics of the song in silence. I knew the words of the song were probably getting to her, and that was exactly what I wanted. After an hour of driving, we pulled up to her place, and she sat staring straight ahead before looking at me like she wanted to say something.

"What's on your mind, baby girl?"

"This can't happen again. You know that, right? Despite what is going on in my marriage, I am still a married woman, and Michael is still my husband, and I can't... won't disrespect him like this. Do you understand?"

I stared at her without cracking a smile, for what I was sure felt like forever to her, before I responded.

"Baby girl, to be honest with you, I don't really give a fuck. Your man hasn't been doing something right because it wouldn't have been so easy to get you in my car if he was. Now I know right now you're struggling with your own conscience, so I'll give you that, but not for long. So don't make me show my ass. Now come here."

She leaned over the console, and I pulled her to me and kissed her until we both had to come up for air.

"I know you got a lot of shit you have to work out with your husband, and I'll give you that time, but not long, you understand?" She nodded her head and opened the door to get out without saying another word to me. I watched her as she walked up the steps and entered the house before pulling off. Ten minutes after dropping her off, I heard my phone go off, alerting me that I had a text.

Baby Girl: *Thank you, dinner at my house tomorrow at 7:00 pm. He'll be there with a guest and I want to even it out so I hope you can make it. Shrimp pasta for us lasagna for them. Hope to see you then.*

Me: *I'll be there, you just be prepared to leave with me.*

I put my phone down and didn't even check her response, because I had no interest in anything she had to say, other than her agreeing to what I said to her. As I continued on my way home, I turned up the music with my thoughts continuing to travel to the evening she and I shared. I glanced in my rearview mirror and noticed a SUV traveling behind me rather closely. I made a few turns to see if it was a coincidence or if this car was following me, but every turn I made, they made as well. Not one to back down from a fight, I slammed on brakes, attempting to get them to hit me, and they stopped just short of hitting my car.

I got out yelling at the driver, telling them to get out of the car, and they just sat there revving the engine without anyone making a move. I couldn't see inside the SUV because it was dark, and the windows were tinted. As I got closer, they backed up so fast the tires squealed, leaving a haze of smoke behind them. I didn't know who these fools were, but first thing tomorrow, I was hitting Tech up. If anybody could find out what was going on, my boy could. Whoever these fools were must not have known who they were fucking with, but they would soon find out, and they would soon regret making a move on me.

10

TRINA

Now after this negro came and showed his ass at my house, he texted me the next day to invite me to dinner at his home so we could all talk.

"Humph. The nerve of this bastard," I said aloud to myself.

"What, Mommy?" my baby asked in all of his innocence.

"Nothing, sweetheart. Mommy was talking to herself. Now finish your breakfast so you won't be late for school."

"Okay, Mommy!"

My son was the best thing to come from that dirty dick bastard, and if it wasn't for him, I would have left well enough alone, but a boy needed his father no matter how much of an asshole that father was. I sat staring at my son, and my mind wandered to the first time I told his father about my pregnancy.

"Get rid of it, because I'm not leaving my wife for you and that little bastard you're carrying"

"No. Don't you see? This means we're supposed to be together—you, me, and our baby?" I said, grabbing his hand and touching my stomach with it. He laughed and snatched his hand away from me with his face balled up in disgust.

"Bitch, my own wife isn't carrying my baby, and you think I'm going to allow you, a known whore, to bring a child, let alone my child, into this world? You must be out of your rabid ass mind. Now get rid of it, or I will," he said to me with his fists balled up and his teeth clenched, so I knew in that moment he didn't give a fuck about me, so I left Florida for a while. I stayed away until I delivered my beautiful baby boy. I looked over at him and smiled, not realizing I was crying until my baby said something.

"Mommy, are you sad?" he asked me, touching my face with his little hand.

"No. What made you ask me that?"

"You're crying. Now who made you sad so I can beat them up?" he asked with his chest stuck out and his little fists balled up as though he was really about to do some damage. I couldn't help but laugh at his attempt to protect me from whatever was bothering me.

"Go get your things so we can go. Mommy is okay. I was just reminiscing on when you were born and realizing how much of a big boy you are, and I got a little sad."

He looked at me with so much innocence and said, "Mommy, I will always be your baby, no matter what, okay?"

"Okay, son. Now go get your backpack so we can go, and remember, you're staying with Nana tonight, okay?"

"Yes!" he said with so much enthusiasm I had to laugh.

"Um, what happened to always being my baby, sir?"

"I am. I'm also Nana's baby too. Plus, she lets me stay up late and have cookies for breakfast because she said that's what grandmas do!"

"Well me and your nana have to have a talk. Now go get ready so we can go."

After dropping my son off to school, I headed over to my favorite salon to allow my beautician to hook me up because I was not about to have dinner with Ronnie and Michael looking ratchet. I had to make sure everything about me was on point, because I was not about to let her one up me like she always did. I knew since I dropped that little bug in her ear about her miscarriages, she was probably balled up in a corner somewhere, unable to function. I laughed to myself because while Ms. Ronnie usually got everything she wanted, or hell, even the things she didn't want, she couldn't have the one thing her heart desired: a baby.

I pulled into a parking space in front of the salon, and it looked like I was the only one here, which meant I would be in and out with time enough to get my nails done. When I walked inside the shop, the normal hustle and bustle that went on here at Marie's on a Friday, was nonexistent. I saw my beautician working on someone, but I couldn't see who it was because the chair was turned away from me, and Marie was standing behind her, working on her hair. I had to admit, Marie had done her thing with her hair. Whoever she was, the bitch had money, because she had on a pair of Louis' that hadn't even been released yet. I knew what they were because I had been trying to get Michael to buy them for me for a while with no success.

"Hey, girl. I'm ready for my makeover," I said, gaining Marie's attention as well as her client, who I definitely wasn't expecting to see. Marie looked at me with a nervous smile, talking as she approached me.

"Hey, girl. You didn't get my message I left this morning asking you to come in this afternoon?" she asked, looking back and forth between me and Ronnie. I looked at Marie, head cocked back and hand on my hip.

"Oh, so this is what we doing now, Marie? I've been coming to you since you were in your momma's kitchen doing hair, and you push me to the side for her?" I said, pointing in Ronnie's direction. She sat in the chair looking at me with a smirk on her face, which pissed me off even more.

"I thought we were friends, but it's apparent that buck stops at the highest bidder."

"Listen, this is business, not personal. I told you I got you this afternoon after I'm finished with my client. Now whatever y'all two got going on ain't got shit to do with me. I will make it up to you, but I got bills to pay, and when she offered to pay me and my clients' money to rent out the shop this morning, I was not passing that up for you or anybody else. Friend or no friend, I don't have a rich baby daddy to pay my bills, so I gotta do what I gotta do to make my money. Now, if you can't respect that, then you can find someone else to do your hair, because I don't have time for the bullshit."

Ronnie continued to smirk and sip her wine as though she got a kick out of the little scene playing out before her, so I looked at Marie and nodded my head and told her I would be back at one for her to do my hair. I headed over to the nail salon that I frequented and was able to get right in the chair. My usual girl told me to sit in the massage chair so she could start on my feet first. I was sitting in the chair with my eyes closed and my glass of wine relaxing, when I heard the door chime from a customer entering the establishment. I didn't look up to see who had entered until I felt someone standing over me. I slowly opened my eyes, and there she was, Ronnie, standing over me staring like she wanted to slit my throat.

"Do you have something to say, or are you just going to stand there staring like an idiot?"

"You just want to be me, huh? You don't have anywhere to go, so you have to visit all of my places. It's not enough you're screwing my husband, but it seems like you want to be me. Get your own life, damn." I looked at her for a minute then burst into an uncontrollable laughter, almost choking on my wine.

"Girl, if you don't get your stuck-up ass out of here with

that bullshit. I think it's you who are used to my leftovers, your husband included. All of these places you frequent, my love, I turned you on to. Even your husband was mine first, but I guess you don't recall all of that, do you?" I placed the mask my nail tech handed me on my eyes and put my headphones in my ear, sipped my wine, and laid my head back, unbothered. She might have run me off from my salon, but if she even attempted to pull that same shit here, she would have a fight on her hands. I felt her walk away, and I smirked, knowing I had gotten exactly what I wanted. I felt my tech getting started on my feet, but she was being rougher than usual.

"Oww!" I screamed, pulling the mask off of my face and looking at my nail tech with a scowl.

"Where is Audrey?" I asked through gritted teeth.

"Um, she had an appointment," the tech stammered out nervously.

"I know she had an appointment, idiot, me! Now where is she? No one touches my feet and nails but her, no offense," I said, craning my neck trying to see if she had gone to the back to get something.

"No. The lady who you were talking to had an appointment with her already, but when she saw you, she said she had everything at her house and Audrey could finish her nails there."

"You've got to be fucking kidding me. OK, who is the next

best in here, because I like my feet, and it felt like you were about to take them off."

"Everyone is booked. Sorry. You should have made an appointment, so it's either me, or you'll have to go somewhere else," the tech said to me with an attitude. After thinking about it for a minute and realizing I didn't feel like driving anywhere else, I gave in and let her do my nails and feet.

"OK, but I swear, if you cut me again, I'm knocking the shit out of you," I said before sitting back in my seat. I hated her even more now. I couldn't wait until tonight to rub my son in her face. I bet she'd cower just like the spoiled brat she was.

"GIRL, THIS IS FIRE!" I said, giving my beautician a hi-five as I turned around in the chair to get a good view of the thirty-six inches she had just installed.

"It almost makes up for you dissing me this morning," I said, rolling my eyes and making a smacking noise with my teeth.

"Well I'm sorry about this morning, but money talks, boo, and I had to get my coins, so no matter what or who is in here, if the money is right, I'd do it again. The only difference is I would call my client before they arrived so they didn't make a blank trip," she said, winking her eye and smiling at me.

"Yeah, yeah, I hear you." I said as I paid her what I owed, and scheduled my next visit. I reminded her she'd better not push me aside for anyone else, or I'd be finding a new stylist and taking my friends with me. I knew I wouldn't hold true to that threat because, whether I wanted to admit it or not, Marie had the best hands on the Treasure Coast and was the only one who could slay my hair like I was about to walk the red carpet. I exited the salon feeling like a million dollars, and knowing I was turning heads made me feel myself just a little more. I threw on my shades and walked to my car, confident in the fact that even if Michael didn't leave with me, he wasn't staying with Veronica, and that made me smile harder than I had in a very long time.

As I stared in the mirror at how good I looked, I couldn't wait to get to this little dinner party with my baby daddy and the missus. I looked down at my slim thick figure, knowing that fat cow Michael laid down with every night could not possibly be keeping his dick hard. I laughed to myself as I grabbed my handbag off the table and strutted to my car, waving at my neighbor Dennis, while praying silently to myself that he wouldn't come over to start a conversation. As I backed out of the driveway, he walked up to my car, signaling me to roll down my window. I rolled my eyes as I obliged him with a fake smile plastered on my face.

"Hey, Dennis," I said through clenched teeth, as he

leaned over in my car smiling with a mouth full of rotten teeth. I swear I threw up in my mouth a little bit at the smell of his breath. One thing about Dennis was he thought because he had a good job and a nice house, he felt he was God's gift to women.

"When are you going to stop avoiding me and let me show you what it is to go out with a real man?" he asked me, showing all three of his good teeth that hadn't turned black or fallen out like the rest of his teeth.

"I'm not sure if I could handle a man of your caliber, Dennis, and I wouldn't deprive the lucky women on the Treasure Coast of all that good love you can provide," I said, trying to keep a straight face.

He smiled hard, believing the line I was feeding him.

"I know that, but I figured I'd make an honest woman out of you and make your son legitimate so he can hold his head up. So what do you say? You going to let me make an honest woman out of you?" I snatched my head around so fast I believe I caught whiplash.

"Well since you want me to be honest with you, you mud mouth bastard, the next time you decide you want to have a serious conversation with someone, make sure you haven't just finished eating an ass sandwich, you Jerome looking motherfucker," I said, rolling my window up and pulling off so fast I almost ran his foot over.

"Stupid bastard," I said under by breath as I drove down the road headed in the direction of Veronica and Michael's house. I wasn't in the mood for any bullshit tonight, so they'd both better realize me coming to dinner was a favor to them both and a chance for me to let my demands be known. I was sick of living in hiding and my son being kept a secret by the one person who was supposed to protect him other than me. If they didn't agree to what I was asking, which wasn't much, I would make their lives a living hell. Yeah, no matter the outcome, tonight was going to be a good night. I looked in the mirror to check my makeup and smiled as I mentally prepared myself for the fireworks I knew that were sure to come once I arrived.

11

VERONICA

As I applied the finishing touches on my makeup, I glanced at the clock and realized it was getting late and everyone should be arriving soon. I put on my clothes and headed downstairs to check on dinner. I checked the sauce for the shrimp pasta, and it tasted divine. I checked the lasagna, and it was almost ready. The cheese was almost that perfect shade of brown you get when mozzarella was baked just right. I called Michel to check to see if he was headed home already. The phone rang several times before going to voicemail, and just as I was about to hang up and call back, I heard the door to the garage opening.

Michael came walking in the kitchen, looking fine as always. He had on a white V-neck t-shirt and a pair of straight legged jeans that hugged his ass just right. It was moments like this, when he walked into a room, making me catch my breath, that made me realize how I fell in love with him in the first place. This man exuded confidence at all times and could catch the attention of any woman so easily, which reminded me of why we were here.

"Where have you been? Out fucking your baby mama?" I asked, voice laced with venom.

"No. I was out grabbing you flowers before I came home. I know how much you like fresh flowers on the table when you have dinner guests, and I felt it was the least I could do after everything I've put you through," Michael said while walking up to me and speaking in a soft baritone. He laid the flowers on the island and headed upstairs to get ready for our little dinner conference.

"Make sure you take a shower and brush your teeth, because while you say you weren't with her, I don't need you getting that bitch's crab laced pussy juice all over my fine China!" I yelled behind him as he walked up the stairs.

I continued giving the staff directions as they finished getting everything prepared for our guests. I heard my phone ding, notifying me I had a text. I looked down and realized it was Jayson telling me he was on his way. Memories of our last night together flooded my mind, and I began to smile at the thought of seeing him again.

"What has you in such a good mood all of a sudden?" my husband asked as he walked into the kitchen after getting dressed.

"My mood status and who is responsible for it, is no longer your concern, nor is it information you will be privy to. Just know it ain't you." I winked at him as I walked out of the kitchen to place the hors d'oeuvres on the table. I dismissed the staff for the rest of the evening as the doorbell rang, and I rushed to the door to answer it, thinking it was Jayson. I was disappointed to find the thot standing there at the door. I slammed the door shut in her face and headed back to the kitchen to finish putting appetizers out for my guest.

"Who was at the door?" Michael asked.

"Thotolina."

"Where is she, in the living room?"

As I opened my mouth to answer his question, the doorbell rang again. Michael got up to answer the door, and I heard him and his baby mom arguing, and I started laughing. I came out of the kitchen when I heard her say fuck that bitch.

"First off, the bitch you fucked is standing in front of you because had it not been for him being such a pussy, we would not be in this position. Now I will attempt to be cordial for the night, but remember, you are in my house, and I have no issues with dragging your ass right out the front door, so do us both a favor and keep the disrespect to a minimum, mkay?" I said, cocking my head to the side with a smirk on my face. I did a Naomi Cambell catwalk, turned, and sashayed my size fourteen ass back into my kitchen, leaving dumb and dumber standing there looking like deer trapped in headlights.

Trina knew how I could get down, because she saw drag a few bitches in college because they mistook me being boujee for being weak. Let's just say the ones who made that mistake once never made it again. I heard the doorbell ring and walked out of the kitchen, checking myself in the hall mirror as I proceeded to the front door to answer it, rolling my eyes at dumb and dumber as I passed. They both seemed to be involved in the same argument they were having earlier, just in a hushed tone. I opened the door and almost forgot my husband was in the room as Jay looked back at me with this huge Cheshire cat grin on his face. It was like time stood still, and it was just the two of us standing in this space.

"What the fuck is he doing here?" Michael asked with a little too much bass in his voice and a scowl plastered on his face.

Jayson just chuckled and leaned over and whispered in my ear, making me adjust my clothes to give me something to do with my hands.

"I'm going to do my best to behave tonight, but the minute your bitch ass husband steps out of line, I'm going to make you cum in front of him just to shut his mouth." He walked over to shake Michael's hand, and Michael looked at it like it had shit on it and walked off. Thotianna didn't waste any time in letting Jayson know who and what she was.

"Well who is this chocolate god that just walked in the door? Ronnie, you didn't tell me you invited a guest. If I had known, I would have gotten dressed up instead of wearing these old rags."

"Bitch, I'm pretty sure your ass spent as much time getting ready as I did in your attempt to prove to my *husband* what he's missing out on, garbage pussy ho."

Jayson burst out laughing and grabbed my hand as we walked to the kitchen.

"So what was that about?" he asked once we reached the kitchen, and he pulled me to him with his arm around my waist, looking down in my eyes.

"Well, Thotianna in there is or was my best friend, my husband's mistress, and baby momma all wrapped up into one, which should make for a fun and exciting evening for all. But I guess I don't have to tell you do I?"

Jayson's eyes got big and a smile slowly spread across his face as he stared directly in my eyes with so much intensity that I became both turned on and uncomfortable at the same time. He seemed as though he was putting thought into what he wanted to say next.

"What?" I asked, voice cracking.

"When we finish this dinner, you're going home with me, and I won't take no for an answer," he said, walking off in the direction of the dining room.

"What have I gotten myself into," I said under my breath.

"That's what I'd like to know," Michael said, making me jump and grab my chest at the sound of his voice.

"You scared me," I said, sounding as though I had just run a marathon. "How long have you been standing there?" I asked, busying myself to distract him from my nervous energy.

"Long enough to see how cozy you and Jay are. So how long you been fucking him?"

I turned my head around to look at this son of a bitch to see if he was serious, because I knew he could be on some bullshit, but this was low, even for his trifling, no good ass.

"First off, the only person I have been fucking is the person I said my vows to. Now just because you and crab pussy in there don't understand the value and significance of marriage vows, doesn't mean that I don't. I just lost our baby, and instead of grieving with my husband, I'm spending tonight having dinner with his baby mama, so the least you can do is indulge my guest. Now grab the lasagna. Dinner is being served," I said, walking off from his stupid ass and heading to the dining room. As I entered the dining room, I saw Thotianna's lack of comprehension was still evident due to the fact she completely ignored my seating chart and was sitting next to Jayson.

"Thoti— I mean, Trina, I see you still struggle with comprehension."

"Huh?" Dumbass looked up at me with her eyes and face scrunched up in confusion.

"Um, your seat is where your name is," I said with a fake smile plastered on my face.

She slowly got up and made her way to her assigned seat and smiled at Jayson.

"I like this view better any way."

He looked over at me, staring me up down, licking his lips and rubbing his hands together as though he was a wolf and I was his intended meal.

"I like my view as well."

Michael walked in, slamming the food on the table, and snatched me up by my arm, pulling me to him.

"I'm not going to have this nigga in my house constantly disrespecting me. Now you check him, or I will." He whispered so hard spit flew from his mouth. I gave Jayson a pleading look with my eyes, and he threw his hands up in mock surrender. All the while, a smirk was plastered on his handsome face.

I sat down in the chair beside Michael and to the left of Jayson, and Trina sat next to Michael, rolling her eyes when he grabbed my hand. He prayed over the food, and I snatched my hand from his grasp as we all began to eat. Jayson grabbed my thigh under the table and squeezed it. The heat that grew between my legs had me gulping air to prevent myself from moaning out loud. I looked over at Michael and grew nervous because he was staring at me as if he knew what was going on under the table. I turned to my plate and started eating my food without saying a word. A devilish grin spread across my face as I got pleasure from watching Michael and Trina devour the very special meal I made just for them. Tonight started off rough, but I had a feeling it was going to end way better than it started, at least for me anyway.

12

MICHAEL

These two kept sitting at the table fawning over each other as though they were the only ones here. I knew she was fucking him, and it was only a matter of time before it all came out. Like my mother always used to say: "What's done in the dark always comes to light."

"I thought we were here to discuss our son," Trina said, looking at me and rubbing on my arm as though my wife wasn't sitting across the table from us. I snatched my arm off the table like someone had just poured hot grease on it. This bitch had no respect, and had it not been for her trout mouth, loose pussy ass, we wouldn't be in this situation in the first place.

"Keep your hands off me. Don't you see my wife sitting here?" I stared at her so hard she nervously looked away and started playing with the napkin in her lap.

"Oh, don't mind me now. I mean, neither of you thought of me while you were fucking and sucking on each other, so why should tonight be any different," she said as a statement more than a question. She lifted her wine glass to her lips. All the while, she had this sinister smile plastered on her face while she watched Trina eating her lasagna. It sent chills up my spine because one thing people didn't know about my wife was that she could go to a very dark place when pushed.

"Look, I know this situation isn't ideal, but what do we do moving forward?" I asked, looking back and forth between both Trina and Veronica, waiting for a response from either of them, but they just sat there staring at each other. Eventually, Veronica broke the silence and looked at me with so much hurt and pain in her eyes. I wanted to make all that happened between us go away. After a minute, she started laughing, and not a ha ha something is funny type of laugh. No, this was a 'women, make sure your wigs are secure, men cover your dicks cause she's about to snap' type of laugh.

"Bitch, what is so fucking funny, huh? You do realize that my son is a permanent part of Michael's life, and the quicker you get out of your feelings about a bunch of dead babies you can't do anything about, the quicker you'll realize that this is a blessing in disguise for you. I mean, you get to be a mommy without all the pain and stress of morning sickness, weight gain, and labor. Well two out of three isn't bad." She looked Ronnie up and down and sipped her wine with a smirk on her face. I just knew at that moment Ronnie was going to lose it, but to my surprise, she was rather calm while Trina continued on her little tirade.

"Hell, I might even let my son call you mommy two or some shit to that effect. I mean, you are his godmother after all, and as long as his father continues to take care of us as he always has, I don't see why we can't be one big happy family, right? I mean, for Jamon's sake."

Veronica sat in silence, not saying one word. Anyone who knew anything about my wife knew that her silence was dangerous.

"I think what Trina is trying to say—" I started to say before Veronica raised her hand, cutting me off midsentence.

"Michael, you don't have to speak for your whore, because it's apparent she has a lot to say, and I want to hear all of it, but before we continue, I want to ask, how was your meal?" We all looked at her confused as fuck. For a minute, I thought she had lost her mind.

"Uh, it was good," Jay-D answered nervously.

"It was good, why?" I answered cautiously.

"Well since we are on the subject of my dead babies, Trina, how is it that you caused my miscarriages, because I am so curious? Please enlighten us."

Trina's ass looked over at me like I was about to save her. She was on her own because her ass wanted to open her big mouth. Now she had to suffer the consequences.

"Bitch, don't look at him. I'm talking to you, not him!" Ronnie screamed while slamming her hand on the table to get Trina's attention, causing the dishes to bang against each other.

"Baby, calm down. We won't get anything solved with you getting so upset," I said, rubbing her arm, and she snatched her hand away, looking at me in utter disgust. Jay-D leaned over and whispered something in her ear, and she immediately calmed down, which pissed me off even further.

"I can't change anything that has happened, but what I can do is ensure the health of myself and my future babies by getting the fuck away from both of you. Oh, and Miss Trina, since you want me to get over my dead babies, you'll both get over it in about the next twenty-four to forty-eight hours. Well, however long it takes the human digestive system to fully digest a meal. Smooches!" she said, starting to get up from the table and blowing a kiss our way.

It took a minute for what she said to register in my brain, as well as for Trina, but once it did, Trina jumped up and ran to the bathroom, making gagging noises, and I grabbed Ronnie by the throat, trying to choke the life out of her. She just looked at me, not smiling or anything, which enraged me even more, causing me to squeeze tighter. Jay grabbed me and pulled me off of her.

"Ain't gon' be none of that fuck shit like that going on while I'm around, so you need to back the fuck up."

"Don't tell me what I can and can't do. This is my wife and my muthafuckin house. Matter of fact, you can get the fuck out,"

I said, running up in Jay-D's face so he would know I meant business. Before we could exchange any more words, Trina came out of nowhere, attacking Ronnie, who was still bent over with her hands on her knees, trying to catch her breath from where I choked her. Trina got a few good licks in before Ronnie got her bearings and laid into her. The way Ronnie had grabbed Trina by the top of her clothes and was wailing on her had both me and Jay-D standing in place with our mouths agape.

The loud thuds that were coming from Ronnie's fists, not open hands, had me wondering if she was temporarily possessed. I must have been in a trance because when I came to, Trina was lying on the ground, knocked the fuck out, while Jay was struggling to keep Ronnie from getting hold of Trina again. Hell, the way all the blood was coming from her face and the knots that were beginning to form had me wondering if the bitch was dead. She started moaning, and it reminded me of Debo from the movie *Friday* when Craig knocked him the fuck out.

"Baby girl, calm down. I'm not letting you catch a charge for a stupid bitch. Now calm your ass down before I have to snatch your lil' thick ass up." Ronnie got quiet for a moment and looked at Jay with a confused look and then she burst out laughing and walked up to him with a devious smile on her face and a hand on her hip as though I wasn't even standing there.

"We both know I am a lot of things, but little isn't one of

them." She turned and looked at me with a look of disgust and hatred all over her face.

"I want you and this garbage out of my house before I return, because right now, I don't want to be anywhere near you." I couldn't even respond. She left me standing there with confusion written all over my face. I looked over at Jay-D, and he had a smirk on his face which had my temperature rising.

"I know you're either fucking my wife or plan on trying to fuck her, either way this between me and her is not over, and believe that this is until death parts us." I stared him straight in his eyes without cracking a smile, and before he could respond, Ronnie came downstairs with a suitcase like she thought this was the end of us.

"Where the fuck you think you going?" I asked Ronnie, grabbing her by the arm in an attempt to make her face me. She snatched her arm from my grip and jumped in my face, eyes squinted, teeth clenched so hard you could see the muscles in her jaw tighten up.

"Wherever the fuck I want to go, and you or nobody is going to check me, boo," she said, pushing my head with her pointer finger as she walked away, giving Trina one final kick.

"And get this bitch out of my house. She's bleeding all over my carpet, and from the looks of her face, she won't be able to make money to get it cleaned. But then again, a whore of her caliber will figure it out, I guess," she said, walking out of the dining room toward what I assumed was the front door, which my assumptions were confirmed when I heard the front door slam. I looked down at Trina and wondered how the fuck this one bitch may have cost me everything. If it wasn't for my son, I would end her life right now. I reached in my front pocket to pull out my cell phone to call 9-1-1 to come take her trifling ass to the hospital, and if she knew what was best for her, she would keep her big mouth shut about everything that went down tonight.

AFTER TALKING to the police about what happened, I headed to the hospital. They didn't believe my story about an intruder, but I didn't give a fuck. I walked into the hospital where Trina was laid up to ensure she wasn't going to do some shady shit like file a report on my wife. Hell, if I had any chance of working things out and trying to fix this situation, I needed to do damage control and quick. I asked the lady sitting at the desk what room Trina was in, and after scanning my ID and giving me a visitor's pass, she proceeded to give me the room number and instructions on how to get to Trina's room.

St. Mary's hospital was a huge hospital, and if you didn't know where you were going, you could easily get lost. The elevator arrived on Trina's floor, and I got off, checking the signs set up along the corridors to ensure I was going the right way. When I got to the hall where Trina's room was, I could hear muffled shouting. As I approached Trina's room, I realized that's where the muffled shouts were coming from. When I walked into the room, I realized why there was shouting. Trina's mother was sitting in the chair next to her bed, arguing with her. Both women got silent as I walked into the room, but the scowl Gloria, Trina's mother wore, verified the conversation they were having was about me.

To say I hated Trina's mother was an understatement. This bitch was always in Trina's ear trying to keep her from fuckin' with me, but the type of emotional and mental control I had over Trina, her mother could never get her to leave me alone, which made her always belittle Trina and constantly put her down. Ms. Gloria couldn't understand how Trina continued to stay with me and even have my child even though I had a wife. What she didn't realize was the more she pushed for her to leave me, the more she pushed her right into my arms.

"Hey, baby. How are you feeling?" I asked as I walked over to Trina's bed and leaned over and kissed her on her forehead, looking at her mother with a smirk on my face.

I would have kissed her on the lips, but Ronnie fucked her up so bad that the only place I could find to kiss her was on her forehead. People often thought because my wife was a socialite, she was a pushover, and it was always a little too late for them when they found out she wasn't.

"Humph. My daughter would be doing better if she wasn't laid up in this bed because of your wife. And do you plan on keeping your son while his mother is laid up in the hospital unable to care for herself let alone her son?" See, this was the shit that irked me with this old bitch; always putting her damn nose where it didn't belong.

"His mother and I will have a discussion about what is best for our son while she is here. I have to take into account how my wife will feel since she knows the truth now."

Ms. Gloria looked back and forth between me and Trina as she slowly stood to her feet.

"I am a good Christian, and I don't like to curse, but you two shits will bring out the worst in anybody. I have sat back and not said anything to you, Michael, but I am putting my foot down. It is not my responsibility to care of Jamon while his mother is laid up because of her stupid decisions. I expect you will be by tomorrow to pick your son up, or I will be dropping him off to your home. You can make this easy or difficult for yourself, so take your pick." She snatched her purse off of the chair she was sitting on and stormed out the door, but not before turning around and looking at me with a final word.

"And you may be able to sweet talk my daughter into giving you what you want, but I'm not her. I expect you tomorrow, or I will visit you at your home." With that, she left the room and slammed the door.

"What the fuck is her problem? Every time we're in the same room, she's always bitchin'."

"Well she's not wrong, you know," Trina said through labored breathing as she tried to sit up.

"Who the fuck side are you on? You know I can't do that to Ronnie, and you were in agreement, so what changed, huh? You still jealous that I married and created a life with her and not you?" I asked, getting in her face.

"N-n-no. I just think a son needs his father, and you are allowing everything to take precedence over your son, and I can't keep letting that slide. My mother's right. You need to spend more time with him."

I let out this maniacal laugh before I stopped and looked at her with all seriousness. I rose from my chair and headed for the door.

"Where are you going?"

I turned from the door and looked back at her.

"If your mother goes through with her plan tomorrow, your cushy life as you know it will end. I will sign over my parental rights, and where do you think that will leave you financially? Handle that by tomorrow morning, or by tomorrow evening, you will be a single parent." I walked out the door and heard a loud scream and something crash against the door. I didn't care how angry she was; she'd better handle her mother, because that shit I said to her wasn't a threat. It was a fucking promise.

13

JAY-D

"Hey, where the fuck you think you going?" I asked baby girl as she made an attempt to put her bags in her car. I snatched the bags from her hand and placed them in my car, and she ran up on me like she was going to hit me. I met her halfway and got in her face and looked dead in her eyes, not caring about the scowl she had on her face.

"I thought we already had this conversation about your hands. Keep mistaking me for your fuck nigga, and I'll show you how a real man gets down. Now I don't believe in hitting women, but I do believe that if you hit, you can get hit back." I stared in her eyes before a smirk spread across my face, and I kissed her on her nose and walked to the passenger side, nodding toward it for her to get in. She kept staring at me, chest heaving up and down like she was on the run with the police hot on her tail. She stood there staring at me like she was contemplating her next move before finally deciding to climb in my car without further complaints.

"Finally, with your hardheaded ass." I closed the passenger side door as she attempted to give me the hotel she thought she would be staying at for the night. I walked around the front of the car and climbed in on the driver's side. I cranked the car up and pulled out of the driveway, ignoring her comment about the hotel, while giving her the side eye and doing my best to keep my eyes on the road at the same time. I turned the music down, and without looking Baby Girl's way, I addressed her.

"Look, I know you're still pissed about ol' girl and your boy fucking around behind your back, but just so you know, we will have a conversation about what went down tonight," I casually said and turned the music back up without another word. Baby Girl swiveled her head around so fast I almost wanted to check to see if her neck was still attached to her spine, because that shit definitely moved a little too loosely for my liking. We continued the car ride in silence until we were about fifteen minutes into our ride, and she realized I wasn't taking her to the destination she requested.

"This doesn't look like the way to the hotel I gave you. Why are we going this way? Please, just take me to the hotel. I just feel the need to be alone tonight," she said, voice cracking. It hurt me to hear the pain and hurt in her voice. I just wanted to make it go away. I refrained from answering her questions, and when she realized she wasn't getting the response she wanted, she turned the music back up, and we continued to ride in silence. We finally arrived at my home, and I pulled onto the driveway and turned the car off. We just sat in silence for a minute. Eventually, I turned around in my seat to face her so I could look directly in her eyes when I spoke to her. I wanted her to hear and feel every word I was about to speak to her. She was staring down at her hands as I gently grabbed her face to turn her head around to face me.

"Tonight, I just want to take care of you... no expectations, no ties, and no bonds. Just you allowing me to be what you want and need for just one night. If you want more, I will give you more. If you want less, I will continue to consume your every thought until you aren't satisfied until you have had more. Can you let me do that for you tonight?"

I stared at her so intensely she began to squirm in her seat and look down at her hands while giving me her answer, barely above a whisper.

"Yes," she said so softly I had to ask her to repeat herself to make sure I heard her correctly. I took her seat belt off with one hand while sliding her over into my lap with the other hand. I stared into her eyes before pulling her in for a kiss. I slipped my tongue into her mouth, and she returned the gesture by gently sucking on my bottom lip. I scooted my chair back so I could turn her to face me, and I placed both of her legs across me in a straddle position. This position had my dick so hard, it felt like it was going to burst out of my jeans to find that wet spot between her legs that was radiating heat. Her pussy was causing my dick to throb so much I was considering just sliding in her, just to satisfy my building curiosity.

I reluctantly pulled away and leaned my forehead against hers as we both did our best to catch our breath and allow our heart rates to go back to normal. I gestured for her to get up so we could get out and go inside before our party began right here in this driveway. I climbed out of the car and reached my hand back in, to help her climb out of the car as well.

"Don't be nervous. I'm not going to hurt you," I said, staring into her eyes with an intensity that had her shifting her gaze so we were no longer making eye contact. After a minute of being shy and withdrawn, a hint of the bold sexy woman I met in her kitchen surfaced. Baby girl walked up to me and got right up in my face with her head cocked to the side and a sly grin on her face.

"I'm not worrying about you hurting me, but I am worried about you being able to let go once you get a taste of these goodies," she said with a smirk on her face before gently taking my bottom lip in her mouth and nibbling on it then sticking her tongue in my mouth. My mans started waking up, and I grabbed her by her hand and started heading to the house, before I snatched her clothes off and started fucking her right here in my driveway.

"What about my stuff? I need my clothes," she said, giggling. I grabbed her hand and placed it on my dick, and she gasped, apparently surprised at the girth, but she recovered real quick and started massaging my man through my pants, which had me seconds away from busting right there, and I hadn't even gotten a feel of the pussy yet.

"Mmm, shit," I moaned, pulling her in for another kiss. I pulled away, looking at her with heavy bedroom eyes.

I swooped her up in my arms, bridal style, and started up the stairs to my master bedroom while kissing her at the same time. I walked into my room and placed her on the bed and stood over her, staring down at this beauty before me. The light from the moon bounced off of her chocolate skin, making her skin glow under the night light.

"Undress," I demanded.

"What?" she asked, looking at me confused.

"Take your clothes off and lay back. And, Baby Girl, don't make me ask you again."

She slowly started undressing herself, and I did the same, while watching her reveal the sexiness she had covered by her clothes. She laid back on the bed, attempting to shield herself from my steady gaze. I climbed on the bed and straddled her, grabbed both of her hands, and moved them off of her breasts. I held her hands down on the bed above her head as I leaned down and kissed her. She started squirming and trying to break free from my hold. I started my trek, planting kisses everywhere my lips ended. I made my way to her breasts and took her nipple in my mouth and circled it, flicking it with my tongue.

"Oh my goodness," she moaned out slowly while arching her back.

"Open your legs," I said with her nipple in my mouth. I started slowly working my way down to that mound between her legs that was currently giving off heat letting me know she was ready for me to explore her center. I slid my hand between her legs, and my hand made its way to her box, where I gently worked the tip of my finger back and forth on her clit, making a waterfall flow between her legs.

"Mmmmh." She softly moaned.

"You like that?" I asked while placing slow deliberate kisses on her neck. She quickly nodded her head yes and opened her legs wider as if to ask me to give her more. I painted soft kisses down the length of her body until I came face to face with her treasure box. I placed a gentle kiss on the tip of her clit, and she raised her ass off the bed as if to increase the pressure of my tongue on her clit. I gently blew air on her pussy, and she grabbed the back of my head, trying to push my face further into it. I moved her hand and looked up at her.

"Please. I need to feel you inside of me," she said, whining and pleading at the same time.

"This is my show, and we do things my way or not at all. Do you understand? Now move your hand again, and I'll go even slower. You understand?"

She nodded her head in frustration, but she followed my instructions completely. I placed my face back in her treasure box and circled my tongue around her clit slowly, while fingering her pussy at the same time.

"Damn, you're wet," I said into her pussy. She just moaned and grabbed the sheets in an attempt to keep her hands off the back of my head. I increased the speed of my tongue, circling around her clit, and her pussy started to pulsate. I knew she was on the verge of cumming, so I pulled my tongue out of her pussy and started to blow on her kitty cat while alternating rolling my tongue around her clit.

"Mmmh, I'm about to cum." I heard her moan barely above a whisper. I struggled to maintain my composure because this woman had me so turned on, I swear I was about to bust right then and there. I looked up at her as I continued to gently suck on her clit.

"Cum for me," I said while inserting two fingers into her pussy while gently making the come here motion at the same time. I felt the wave of her orgasm begin to take over as her pussy tightened around my fingers, and her juices squirted all over me. I continued to lick her juices up while her body continued to convulse, as wave after wave of orgasms continued to hit her. I stood at the foot of the bed, stroking my dick and watching as she came down off the high I put her on. She looked up at me with a lazy grin, looking sexy as fuck, with her hair sprawled out all over the pillow and the moonlight bouncing off her chocolate skin, making her have a soft blue hint to her skin. I leaned over and started kissing her so she could taste herself on my tongue, she attempted to take control of the situation by reaching for my mans. I looked at Baby Girl and smirked.

"Nah. Tonight is all about you. Lay back and enjoy the ride."

I laid her back down on the bed and took my knee and spread her legs apart as I slowly rubbed my fingers across her clit, feeling the river between her legs starting to flow again. I positioned my mans against her opening, and she gasped before I could do anything.

"You ready for this? Because once I start, ain't no stopping." She slowly nodded and spread her legs wider, giving me permission to enter her sweet spot.

"Ssss, oh fuck!" I moaned in her ear and started kissing her more aggressively. I knew I told her there were no expectations, but the way she was feeling, I was lying to myself if I felt I could stay away from her. I started off with long, deep, slow strokes, attempting to touch her throat. She matched me stroke for stroke. My toes started to curl, and I knew I was coming close to reaching my peak, so I had to do something because I wasn't going out like that.

I took her legs and placed them together over her head with her feet touching each other. I slammed into her pussy, slow and hard, only pulling out to the tip, and slammed back into her pussy deeper than the time before.

"Aww fuck, Jay! S-slow down, baby. I'm about to cum again," she said, her pussy beginning to tighten its grip on my dick, forcing my mans to swell even more. My nut was building, and I knew it wouldn't be long before I blew my seeds all up in her inviting womb. I sped up the pace, and before I knew it, we were both releasing at the same time. She squirted all over me, and I planted my seeds all up and through her pussy. I tried to pull out, but she had a grip so tight on my dick I couldn't move.

"Fuck, girl. That shit between your legs is lethal!" She looked over at me and burst out laughing.

"I don't know what you laughing at. Got a brotha over here ready to add your name to the bank account, businesses, and deeds. Hell, your ass had me over here damn near screaming like a lil' bitch. Toes curling and all." I was looking at her so seriously she almost fell out the bed because she was laughing so hard. She turned on her side to snuggle up under me with her head on my shoulder. I was laying on my back with my hands behind my head, so she had to turn her head to look up at me when she talked.

"Thank you."

"For what?" I asked, knowing the answer but needing to hear her say it.

"Thank you for everything. I needed tonight, and while I still have some healing to do, tonight erased all my problems from my mind for just a minute."

She turned to look at me with her head resting on her arm that was on my stomach.

"You got a sista out here ready to add your name to her business, bank accounts, deeds, and the will," she said with a smirk on her face. We held each other's gaze before she got a sneaky grin on her face and started to slowly lower her face between my legs. She left a trail of kisses from my mouth to my dick, which was apparently her intended destination. Baby Girl slowly started to take my dick in her mouth, swirling the tip of my dick with her tongue while forming a sucking motion with her mouth. She slowly started to bob her head up and down, continuing with the slight sucking motion, when she pulled up, making my toes curl each time she reached the tip. She drooled down my dick, getting it nice and wet. As she started using her hand to stroke my dick, she used her mouth to suck both of my balls into her mouth at the same time, twirling her tongue around my balls. Baby girl started to do this humming thing with her throat, and I almost nutted right then and there. My toes curled up, and I had to lift my head to stare at this woman in awe when she started alternating between humming and twirling her tongue around my shit. I swear I almost nutted right then, because I had never had no shit done to me like that before.

"Ah fuck, girl. You are gonna make me cum." She slowly lifted her head and looked at me with this soft, sultry look on her face. She took her tongue and slowly started licking from my balls, like she was licking an ice cream cone, all the way to my dick. When she got to what must have been her final destination, she deep throated my shit, all the while staring me dead in my eyes, which was driving my ass crazy. I snatched her up and slammed my dick inside her so hard and fast from the back. Her pussy muscles clenched my dick so tight I couldn't move.

"Ummm, fuck! I'm cumming."

"Give me that." I leaned over and whispered in her ear as I slowly started working my way in and out of her, and her kitty cat started leaking down my dick.

I pulled back so I could watch my dick, which was glistening from her juices. I was gliding in and out of her, and all you could hear were her soft moans which made me go in even harder. Baby Girl had the softest and sexiest moans, which made me want to fuck her all night, but I knew I was on the edge of what could possibly be the biggest nut in my life. I turned baby girl over so I could look deep in her eyes.

"The way your pussy is clenching my dick, I know ya man ain't fucked you good in a while, but baby girl, your pussy got me on the edge. So when I tell you I'm going to cum, you better cum with me. Can you do that for me, Baby Girl?"

She nodded her head.

"Nah, I'mma need to hear you say that shit out ya mouth, because if you cum before I tell you to, I'm going to have to fuck you till you can obey. You understand?"

"Ahhh, yes!" she moaned. "I can't hold it much longer, Jayson!"

"Hold that shit till I tell you." I felt her pussy begin to pulsate around my dick, and I knew I couldn't hold on any longer, and neither could she.

"You ready?" She started nodding her head and quickly remembered my order.

"Yes, yes, oh yes!"

"Then gimme that shit!" I whispered in her ear, and we both let go at the same time.

"Ahhhh fuck!" I screamed all the while staring her dead in her eyes. We both had to take a moment to catch our breath because we were both beat. I grabbed her around her waist, holding on tight as I turned over on my back while still inside her. We both started dozing off with me rubbing my hands up and down her back.

"Jayson," she started.

"Shhh. You don't have to say anything. I told you no expectations, and while I want more, I know you're not ready for that. Just know I'm here for you."

"Mmm, okay," she said, sounding as though she was already asleep. Hell, listening to her breathe was so calming, my ass was knocked out in no time, with the hope that this wouldn't be it for us.

I WOKE up the next morning to the smell of bacon and the sound of pots clanging, and I decided to get up, take a shower, and get dressed so I could see what was going on downstairs. After I finished taking care of my hygiene, I got ready and headed downstairs, hoping it was Baby Girl and not my chef. As I was walking down the steps, I heard Beyoncé and someone's off key attempt at singing "1+1."

I stood in the doorway of the kitchen, watching her as she danced around the kitchen, singing and cooking like she didn't have a care in the world. She obviously made herself at home because she was standing there with one of my t-shirts on, which appeared to be all she was wearing, because every time she moved, all you could see were her ass cheeks. I walked up behind her and put my arms around her waist and pulled her to me as I placed my head in her neck and inhaled her scent.

"Mmmm, you smell good. Good morning."

She turned around and wrapped her arms around my neck and kissed me so passionately, my mans began to slowly rise.

"Thank you for last night. I needed it more than you know."

"Trust me, the way malady was gripping my shit last night, I know just how badly you needed what I gave you last night, and if you keep moaning like you just did with that little shit you got on, we'll have a repeat of last night right here in the kitchen."

"Well let me back up, because I got some things I need to straighten out with you know who, so while I appreciate what you did for me, I still have things I need to work out before we take it there. Can you understand that?"

I moved closer to her and pulled her into my arms and looked her in her eyes.

"I told you last night there were no expectations. This was about you. Would I be lying if I said I didn't want more? Yes, but I know you had a situation before last night happened. Just know that I'll be patient for so long before I make what I want known. If you can understand that, then we're cool." I pecked her on her forehead and walked over to the stove to see what she made, and she popped my hand and told me to sit down, and she would bring me my plate. I sat at the table, and she brought me a plate of grits, scrambled eggs, turkey bacon, homemade biscuits, and a plate of fresh fruit. Instead of sitting down and eating with me, she started cleaning the kitchen.

"Leave it. My cleaning lady will be here. She'll take care of all of that. I have to go to work. Are you staying here until I get off?"

"No. I better get home and do damage control. Michael's ass is probably on the war path this morning, so I might as well deal with that headache and get it over with, but thanks for the offer. I'll get ready while you finish eating."

"If that's what you want, I'll drop you off on my way to work."

I watched her as she headed upstairs, all the while hoping she would be able to walk away, because if not, revenge would have to take the back seat, and I just might have to murk Michael's ass to get what I wanted.

14

VERONICA

As I rode next to this gorgeous man who made me feel like a queen last night, a wave of guilt washed over me. I knew that Michael did me wrong, but I couldn't come to terms with two wrongs not making a right, and I felt even worse. I would be lying to myself if I didn't somewhat feel good about the revenge though. A small smile had creeped up on my face as I thought back to last night and how good Jayson made me feel.

"What are you smiling about?" he asked, taking my left hand in his and kissing the back of it, which caused me to shiver and my girl to start betraying me.

"Are we going to start lying to each other?" he asked as he slipped his hand under my dress, and he slid a finger into my pussy, making me moan out loud.

"Just like I thought. You were thinking about last night.

You might be able to lie to me, but malady will always give you away," he said, winking at me with that one dimpled smile that always kept me blushing.

"OK, I was thinking about last night, wishing it didn't have to end so quickly."

Scrrreech.

"We can turn around right now and go back to my place. All you have to do is say the word." This fool had stopped in the middle of traffic and was dead serious. I burst out laughing at the serious look he had on his face. Once I got myself under control, I told him to take me home before we got into an accident, and neither one of us would have a chance at sampling the goods again.

"I'm just saying, don't be saying stuff like that to a brother, because we may not ever leave the house again."

"You are crazy, you know that, right?" I laughed.

"Only for you," he said with a serious look on his face while attempting to keep his eyes on the road and look at me at the same time.

We finally pulled up to my house, and I noticed Michael's car was still in the driveway.

"Ugh. He hasn't left for work yet. I thought I would have time to gather my thoughts before having to deal with this fool, but I guess not."

"You want me to go in with you, just in case he tries some funny shit with you?"

"Nah, he won't try me like that, because he doesn't want

to have to deal with my father." I leaned over and kissed him as I got out of the car to grab my things from the back seat. I closed the passenger side door and leaned in the window and told him that I would call him later. I watched as he pulled out of the driveway, trying to avoid the much-needed conversation I needed to have with my husband. I walked in the front door and went straight to the kitchen, walking through the dining room—which had been cleaned up and everything put back in its place like nothing had happened—where I heard talking. I saw Michael sitting at the table, reading the paper and drinking his coffee, and our maid, Ms. Ann, washing dishes.

"Good morning, Ms. Ann. Can you give me and Michael a minute, please?"

She nodded her head, turned the water off, and dried her hands to head upstairs, but not before stopping to give me a hug and whispering in my ear.

"Do what makes you happy, and don't let anyone deter you." She held me at arms' length before heading upstairs to clean.

"Michael—" I started, but he cut me off before I could finish.

"No need to apologize. I did what I did, and you got your little revenge fuck, so let us just forget about it all and move on. I forgive you. Now go wash that nigga off of you and come have coffee with your husband before he has to go to work."

I looked at this man with wide eyed confusion. I mean, I felt as though I was living in *The Twilight Zone.*

"Am I on fuckin' Candid Camera. I mean, is Ashton Kutcher going to jump out and punk me, because I feel like I am in some real alternate reality type bullshit right now."

"Watch your mouth. That is no way for a lady of your caliber to speak. I mean, one night of fuckin' a thug and you come home acting like a real hood rat."

"I guess good dick will do that to you," I said, cocking my head to the side with a smirk on my face.

"Why didn't you tell me I could have a fucking orgasm on a dick without having to play with my pussy? I mean, he fucked me so good I not only came on his dick, but I sucked it as well, and I loved it!" I knew that would get under his skin, because the entire time we'd been married, I never sucked his dick. I guess all the fucking around he did really turned me off. Hell, being burned would do that to you.

We were staring hard at each other, and I saw the anger flash in his eyes and the little vein on the right side of his neck pulsating, which had me a little nervous. I started laughing because I knew if Michael was white, he would be beet red.

"What the fuck did you just say to me?" he asked, coming close to me with a deranged look in his eyes which had me regretting what I had just said, but I couldn't back down now; I was at the point of no return.

"You heard what the fuck I said. That man gave me more

pleasure in one night than you have in our entire marriage, and I fuckin' loved it. I can still taste him on my tongue." I closed my mouth and let out a slight moan like I was reminiscing about Jayson touching me.

"Is that right?" he asked, laughing. It scared me because it wasn't a laugh from humor but that of someone on the verge of losing what little sense they had left. It was an 'I'm about to do some serial killer type shit' laugh. I grabbed a knife from the sink and waited for his next move.

"Well since we're being honest and laying all our cards out on the table, let me hit you with some real shit. I met Trina before you and continued to fuck her our whole relationship. I guess you could say no other pussy gripped my shit like hers. And check this out. This is the real kicker. When you miscarried our first child, I purposely got her pregnant to keep her happy and her mouth shut. But since we laying all of our cards out on the table, you want to know what the real joke is, and I think you gone like this shit?" he asked, sounding like a deranged lunatic. He leaned over real close to my ear so only I could hear.

"I helped her give you the medicine so you would miscarry." He whispered so hard spit flew from his mouth.

I was stunned. I mean, I was in complete and utter shock. I slid down to the floor with my mouth wide open and just sat there, staring off into space as he drank the last of his coffee and put his jacket on to leave for work.

"Is there anything else?" I asked in a monotone voice

which should have sent up red flags for him, because I was a little too calm.

"Yeah. You need to thank your father for me marrying you. Had it not been for him and his connections, you would probably be a spinster waiting for someone to come along and dust your pussy off." He looked down at me with such disdain and disgust, something in me snapped.

"Arghhhh." I jumped up, running toward him with my knife raised, wanting to cut his fucking soul from his chest. We struggled for a minute before he threw me to the floor and snatched the knife from my hands, but not before I nicked his arm.

"You stupid bitch! You cut me!" He snatched the knife from my hand and slammed it in the sink while checking the cut on his arm. He could be such a bitch. I didn't know what I ever saw in him.

"I... hate... you, and you're lucky your arm is the only thing I cut," I said, chest heaving up and down and sweat running down my face like I had just run a marathon.

"You smug, selfish bastard, I gave you everything, and this is how you repay me? If I wasn't convinced I was done before, I know I am done now. But know this; I am not done with you, and before all of this is done, you will feel my wrath one way or another."

I got up off the floor and headed upstairs to my bedroom to take a shower and get his shit out of my house. As I turned the shower on, I heard the alarm to the front door, alerting me that the door had opened and closed, and I figured it was Michael leaving for work. I went to the window to look out, and I saw he had changed shirts. I smirked at the thought of the look on his face when I pulled the knife on him.

I went into the bathroom to get my shower so I could get started on my plan to make Michael pay for every ounce of pain I was feeling. After getting out of the shower and getting dressed, I called a locksmith to come change the locks. I also called the security company to change all of the passwords and security codes to the security system. I finished getting dressed and grabbed my keys to head out to get my day started, and my next stop was the bank. I was taking my name off all of his accounts as well as taking everything I put in our joint accounts. I was going to show this bastard I wasn't the one to play with. This bastard and his bitch cost me my children, and I was going to make their asses pay, but Michael first.

As I walked out of the bank after taking my name off of all of Michael's accounts and removing the money I put in the accounts, leaving just enough to get himself something to eat off the dollar menu, I hopped in my car to head to the mall for some retail therapy. My phone rang, and I looked at my dashboard in the car to see that it was Jayson calling. A smile spread across my face as I answered his call.

"Hey, sexual chocolate. How is your day going?" He laughed that deep throaty laugh that had my panties wet just from the sound of it.

"Good. I haven't made it to the office yet. I had a few meetings outside of the office, and I was headed that way, and I decided to call you to see if you wanted to get some lunch. I mean, if you and ya man ain't made up yet."

"Somebody sounds jealous," I said, laughing.

"Nah, you belong to me, so I'm not worried because, like I told you this morning, malady will tell on you every time. She only gets wet for me. I made sure of that last night when I signed my name on her with my tongue. Just like now, stop clenching your legs and breathe. I'll take care of that when I see you."

I didn't even realize I was holding my breath until he said something, and how did this man know I was turned on just from the mere sound of his voice? I didn't know how I was going to control myself around him.

"You know your silence just gave you away, right?" He laughed that sexy, deep throated laugh like Idris Elba.

"I plead the fifth," I said, attempting to avoid the truth. "Do you want to meet up at The Cheesecake Factory?"

"Yeah. That's near my office. And Ronnie, keep her wet for me."

This man hung the phone up so quick I couldn't even respond, but whatever he was doing to me had me experiencing feelings I had never felt before, which had me blushing.

I arrived at the Cheesecake Factory and was seated right away due to it being the end of the lunch hour rush. Jayson walked up looking like he'd just stepped off the cover of a magazine, and I got chills. I saw how all of the women in the restaurant were attempting to make eye contact with him, yet he only had eyes for me. I blushed as he came over to the table and grabbed my hand for me to stand so he could give me a hug.

"Mmmmh!" I moaned without realizing it, but the feeling I had while in his arms had me feeling at ease after the morning I had with my soon to be ex-husband.

"I missed you." He whispered in my ear, making me shudder from the warmth of his minty breath against it. I pulled away from him and busied my hands, fixing my clothes in an attempt to hide the nervous and excited feeling I had every time this man was near me. We sat down at the table, and Jayson waved the waitress over and asked if we could be moved to a booth, and she took one look at this Morris Chestnut chocolate god and agreed, all the while cheesing like a Cheshire cat.

"Do you have that effect on all women?"

He looked at me, eyebrows furrowed in confusion, as we got up to follow the waitress to our new seat.

"What effect?" he asked from behind me.

I stopped walking and turned to face him so I could look in his eyes as I answered his question.

"The effect that dimpled smile and rugged good looks has on women when you look their way and smile. The look that has them saying, in so many words, 'have your way with me, daddy.' There is not a woman in here that has not tried to get your attention since you walked through the door."

He looked around the restaurant as I continued to our booth and sat down. The waitress, who apparently had no respect for my presence, continued to gawk and wait for Jayson as though I wasn't sitting here. When he arrived at the table, he sat down next to me with a smirk on his face as though it just dawned on him what I was saying.

"Is there anything you need?" she asked him, insinuating she wanted more than to take our lunch order. Before I could say anything, Jayson grabbed the back of my neck and pulled me in for a kiss so deep and passionate I almost forgot where we were. We caught our breath before he turned to look at her with a smirk on his face.

"Unless you got a room back there where I can relieve these uncontrollable urges I have whenever I'm with my girl, then nah, we good. We'll give our food order in a minute."

She sucked her teeth as she walked off and we both looked at each other before laughing out loud at how embarrassed she must have felt.

"I think your friend is mad."

"I don't give a fuck about what any woman is this room

thinks about me but you. Do you understand that?" he asked, staring at me with such an intensity I had to look away.

"Veronica, look at me."

I slowly turned my head to face him, and we continued to stare in each other's eyes as though we were the only two in the room.

Jayson started using his right hand to massage my thigh, still holding the stare that had me captivated. When he started slowly creeping his hand up my thigh to my warm center, I grabbed his hand in an attempt to stop him, and from the way he scrunched up his face and shook his head, I knew that was a mistake, and he was going to have his way whether I agreed or not.

"You have one of two options: You can allow me to continue what I'm doing without anyone knowing what I'm doing, or I can duck under the table and have you screaming in no time. Now one of those options will be a dead giveaway to what I'm doing. So which will it be?" he asked, looking at me without cracking a smile.

After a short deliberation, I removed my hand from his and allowed him to reach his destination. I jumped and let out a soft moan because he had somehow snuck an ice cube in his hand without my knowledge, and he was currently rubbing it against my clit which was feeling so good. I had my eyes closed and letting out what I thought were soft moans until Jayson informed me otherwise.

"Ssssh, Baby Girl, or you're going to get us kicked out of

here. Maybe I should have gone under the table," he said, letting out a soft chuckle. Just as I was about to have another soul shattering orgasm, my phone rang.

"Hello!" I answered, feeling so relaxed you would have thought I had just smoked a blunt. Jayson continued to work his magic on my pussy as I slowly grinded against his hand, trying to keep my focus on the phone call.

"What the fuck did you do?" I was having such a feeling of euphoria that it took me a minute to register who I was talking to. When I realized who it was, I quickly came down off of my high.

"Are you fucking stupid?" I had to pull the phone away from my ear and look at it in sheer disgust, because the person on the other end was surely about to get cussed the fuck out.

"Who is this?" I asked with a look of confusion on my face.

"Oh, you spend one night fucking the next nigga and you can't remember your husband's voice? Hell, do you even remember you're a married woman?" Michael asked, voice laced with venom.

"Didn't we already establish this morning that good dick will have you doing some crazy things? I guess forgetting your voice is one of those things to add to the list. Now what do you want?"

"I guess good pussy will do that too. Maybe that's why I

continued to fuck Trina, but that's not why I called. Did you do something to the accounts?"

"Ohhhh, that!" I laughed.

"Don't fucking play with me. Did you change the fuckin' accounts or not?"

"Yes, and the way I see it, you owe me for the wasted years, time, and energy I put into what is obviously a dead relationship. You will not take a dime of my money and spend it on that whore and her son, so the way I see it, we're even. Y'all two are going to have to figure that shit out without my money. Deuces!"

I ignored his pleas and hung the phone up in his ear.

"Now where were we?" I asked Jayson, but his phone rang at the moment I turned to give him my undivided attention. He put his finger up for me to give him a second, so I started to order our food while he had what seemed to be a tense conversation with someone on the phone. I heard him tell whoever was on the phone he was headed to the office, and he would meet them there. He hung up the phone and pulled me in for a kiss and an embrace.

"I've got to go; an emergency has come up at work, but I want you to have lunch on me, and we'll finish what we got started here later."

"I understand. I'll meet you at your place later," I said, feeling slightly disappointed but not showing him so he wouldn't feel bad about leaving me here to eat alone. It was times like this that

I missed my best friend, until I remembered her betrayal, then that nostalgic feeling would leave as quickly as it came. I sat here eating my lunch, realizing how quickly my life had changed and how my future relied solely on the decisions I made moving forward. I made up in my mind that it didn't matter how much money I took from Michael, I had to create my own future, and moving forward, that was exactly what I was going to do.

15

MICHAEL

Veronica really didn't know what she had done. Imagine my surprise when I showed up to the bank to do my monthly withdrawal, and my accounts were empty, except a couple thousand dollars in each account. I mean every single fucking account had been drained of everything except a couple thousand dollars. I guess she was trying to be funny, but I didn't see shit funny in her actions. This bitch didn't realize the money she took doesn't belong to me or her, and if I didn't figure out how to get it back from her, we were both going to suffer the consequences.

I knew the Damian brothers were into some shady shit while I was working with them, but I didn't know the depths of their criminal activity until the shit hit the fan when Jay-D bought the business from under them. I realized the money they had me dropping off every month was money he had been cleaning through the business for the Mexican Cartel, and now my stupid wife was about to get us both killed on her vendetta shit. I had to get that money back, and I had no idea, at this moment, how I was going to do that.

"Fuck!" I yelled, and everyone in the bank turned their heads to look at me like I had lost my damn mind, and being the only black man in the building didn't help. I rushed out the building, pushing the door open so hard it almost slammed back in my face with the same force. I got in the car, slammed the door, and sped off. I was driving around town, with no particular destination in mind, when my phone rang. I looked at the caller ID and it was an unfamiliar number, so I didn't bother picking up. Immediately after the call ended, another call came through from the same unknown number, and I slid the red button to the left, sending them to voicemail. After doing this several times and the caller not getting the hint, I answered the phone, frustrated.

"Who the fuck is this?" I asked, ready to cuss out whoever was on the other line acting like they didn't understand what not answering the phone meant.

"Mr. Boudreaux, you are a very hard man to find." This soft, sexy voice with a Spanish accent came through on the other line, almost making me forget I was angry at whoever was calling.

"Well if reaching me is such a task, it must mean I don't want to talk or be found, but I guess some people don't understand that shit." The mystery caller let out a soft chuckle, and there was a short bout of silence before she offered a response to my statement.

"I'll let that little comment go since it's evident your bosses didn't explain to you who I am, but make no mistake. That is the one and only time I will allow you to slide with the little slick comments. Now what did your bosses tell you about our little business arrangement?" she asked, causing me to become more confused than I was when I answered the phone.

"Lady, you have about thirty seconds to explain who you are and why the fuck you are ringing my line asking me about my former bosses. I don't have time to play games, and I'm about two seconds from ending this call if you don't give me any answers."

I didn't know who this bitch was, but she was definitely pissing me off the more she talked and continued to avoid my questions.

"Who I am is none of your concern; however, what you were supposed to have and deliver to me today is my concern. I hope you are not trying to take off with my money as your friends the Damien brothers have done, Mr. Boudreaux, because that would be a bad idea for both you and that beautiful son of yours and his mother. We wouldn't want them having an, how do you say, umm unfortunate incident that would remove them from your life permanently." The way this woman spoke in such an eerily calm and soft tone had me just a little shook, but I couldn't let on that she was getting under my skin.

"Bitch, if you knew anything about me, you would know killing them would be doing me a favor and is not a threat. Hell, kill 'em. You'd be doing me a solid getting rid of both of they asses, no child support or black mail money. I'll even give you their locations to make the job easier. Now if that'll be all, I got shit to do," I stated, about to end the call until I heard Ronnie's name.

"What the fuck did you just say?" I asked, putting the phone back up to my ear.

"You heard me, Mr. Boudreaux. I wonder if you would feel the same if it were your wife, Veronica? Hmmm, I wonder if she would even see it coming."

Ding.

I heard a notification on my phone.

"You might want to check that," she said as though she could hear my notifications go off. I pulled the phone from my ear and glanced down at the screen and saw that I had a text message come through. I opened the text message, and it was a video of Ronnie getting in her car at the valet station in front of The Cheesecake Factory. Whoever was working the booth must have been working for the mystery woman on the line, because the video was so close I could almost smell her perfume through the phone.

"You see, everyone has a weakness, and I make it my business to know what that weakness is. Now do you understand me?" she asked as I put the phone back to my ear.

Whoever sent the video to my phone had me nervous as fuck, because I had no idea who this woman was or what she was capable of.

"What do you want?" I asked through clenched teeth and holding the phone in my hand so tight, my knuckles looked like they had doubled in size.

"Oh, I guess I have your attention now, huh? What I want is the money you were supposed to drop off to the designated location earlier today. You see, the Damien brothers are for some reason unreachable, so that leaves you, their flunky, to get me my money," she said in her thick, heavy accent.

"I need my money by the end of the day tomorrow, or I have a feeling you will be making arrangements of a different kind Mr. Boudreaux. I hope we have a clear understanding moving forward, sir."

Before I could respond to her statement, I heard several beeps, indicating the call had ended.

"Fuck me! How the fuck am I supposed to get that type of money with Veronica acting stupid as fuck."

I rode around town for a few minutes before turning around in the middle of the street to head back to the office. If I couldn't get the money myself, maybe convincing Jay-D paying this money is the only way to keep Ronnie safe will have him donating to the cause. Hell, I might even pad the number to get a little for myself. He wanted to be her man, then he could keep her ass safe and pay me for my pain and suffering of losing my wife as well.

As I walked into the office, Margie was sitting her ass at the front desk, looking evil as fuck. I hated her ass, and she definitely hated me. After everything that went down in the conference room, I knew her ass was plotting for my demise.

"Good afternoon, Mr. Boudreaux. I placed your mail on your desk, and Mr. Smith called looking for you. He said to call him as soon as you got in," she said as I walked in through the front door.

"Yeah, when I feel like it," I mumbled, thinking she wouldn't hear me.

"What was that?"

"I said right away, and thank you."

"Oh, you're welcome," she said with what I could have sworn was a smug grin on her face.

I walked into my office and checked my messages. As my computer started up, my phone rang, and I contemplated not answering that shit 'cause I already didn't want to be here today.

"Hello."

"Come to my office."

Click!

"I know this punk ass nigga did not just call my phone and hang up on me. Bitch ass, " I said as I got up to head to his office to see what the fuck he wanted. I entered his office and sat down across from him as he finished up a phone call.

He turned his back, and I heard him say keep that shit wet for daddy, and I'll take care of her when I get home. *I know he's not talking to my wife*, I thought to myself. He got quiet for a few moments, listening to whoever was on the other end of the call.

"I gotta go. I'll see you when I get home," he said, ending the call. He turned around in his chair and shuffled some paper without looking at me or saying a word.

"Well damn, how many ladies you got?" I asked so I could let Ronnie know she wasn't as special as she thought.

"One. Her nigga wasn't hitting that shit right, so she's calling me daddy now," he said with a smug grin on his face before addressing why I was here.

"Look, I called you in here because I'm trying to figure out about these large deposits and withdrawals from the company account in your name. Were the brothers aware of this activity, or were you stealing company funds?"

I stared at him, contemplating whether I was going to just walk up out of here for him questioning me or actually answer his question. I decided to do a combination of both.

"Look, anything I did was overseen by the Damien brothers, so maybe you need to direct your questions at them."

I stood up and was opening the door to walk out, when he caught my attention with his last statement.

"I would if I could, but they were found dead, along with their wives, in the Maldives. The report says their hands were cut off and their bank accounts emptied. If you know anything about what they were into, I need to know 'cause I'm not trying to run into any surprises."

"Nah. I don't know about anything they were into," I said and walked out of his office, slamming the door behind me. When I got back to my office, I pulled out my cell phone and called the unknown number from earlier with the hopes that the mystery woman would pick up.

"You have my money already?" she asked when she answered the phone.

"No, but I have a plan to get it, but I'm going to need your help."

She got quiet, contemplating what I just said before answering.

"Okay, but know if this is some type of trick, you'll be dead before you can get out of your car. Meet me in one hour at The Cheesecake Factory." She once again hung up without another word.

I sat back in my chair with a huge grin on my face, because if my plan worked the way I wanted to, I would have two headaches out of my life without having to put in any work, and I would be rich with little effort. My mind drifted to Trina, so I decided to give her a call to see if she had been released from the hospital yet and to gauge what she was thinking when it came to whether or not she was planning to press charges. I dialed her number, and her phone rang a few times before she picked up.

"Michael, what do you want?" she asked in a raspy, tired sounding voice.

"I just called to check on you and see how you were feeling; I can't do that now?"

She let out a long sigh as though the sound of my voice irritated her now.

"Michael, after what went down with your wife, the only thing you and I need to be focused on is our son. I can't go there with you and you break my heart once again."

I pulled the phone away from my ear and stared at it because this did not sound like the woman that would do anything for me. This couldn't be her speaking. It sounded as though her trifling ass, no man keeping mamma had gotten in her head and was speaking for her.

"So what, you don't love me now? Is that it?"

"Michael, this isn't about how I feel about you but more about how you feel about me."

"I'm coming by, so be ready when I get there."

I hung up the phone before she could respond to my statement. I had already lost my wife, and Trina was my go-to, and I couldn't lose her too. I was going to stop by the mall and pick her up something on my way to her house. That should do the trick and get me back in her good graces. I picked her up a new Louis Vuitton bag and some Louis Vuitton shoes, and just in case our son was home, I grabbed him a shirt with one of the characters I remembered he liked. An hour later and I was pulling onto

Trina's driveway, and as I parked, I noticed her mother's car in the driveway. This bitch just always had her ass involved in something that wasn't her business. I smiled to myself as I got out of the car and grabbed all the stuff I picked up for her and my son. When I got to the door, it swung open before I could ring the doorbell or knock. Her mother stood before me with her teeth clenched and her face balled up in a scowl.

"What the fuck are you doing here?" she asked while my son tried to get around her to hug me. She kept holding him back as he struggled to get around her to get to me.

"First off, who the fuck are you talking to? This is my house, and I should be asking you what the fuck you doing here."

"Doing the job you should be doing while your son's mother is unable to care for him, ya sorry bastard."

"Well I'm here now, so you can go and take that stank ass, hood rat attitude and get the fuck out," I said, almost knocking her over as I walked into the house, giving my son his gift and giving him a big hug and a kiss. He was cheesing from ear to ear as though I had given him a million dollars. Trina's mother stood at the front door with a scowl on her face and the door wide open like I was going to leave. Her attempt at keeping me out was futile. Hell, my name was on this shit, and if Trina didn't like me here, she could pack her shit and go back to the hood right 'long with her nappy head, horse face ass mama.

"Are you staying here tonight, Daddy?" my son asked,

looking at me with the most innocent look on his face. It was times like these that made me want to stop all the foolishness and be what my son and Trina needed me to be. However, my ambitions to do and be more was too great to give in to what they needed. Hell, call me selfish, but I wanted it all, and if my plan went the way it was supposed to, I would still have it all, including the connections from Veronica's dad.

"We'll see, son. Right now, I need to talk to your momma, so can you go play in your room while we grownups talk?"

"You're not going to make her cry again, are you?" he asked innocently which made me wonder what the fuck Trina had been telling my son behind my back.

"No, son, now go play."

BAM!

Trina's mom slammed the door so hard I thought she was going to tear it off the hinges. She walked by me with a smirk on her face she passed by me going up the hallway and stopped when she got near the kitchen and turned around to face me and had a look on her face like she was gonna say something, but she must have changed her mind and kept going and disappeared in the spare bedroom. I swear I was sick of this woman's bullshit.

"Trina!" I yelled as I walked into the kitchen to get me something to drink. I heard a bedroom door open, and I heard her footsteps slowly coming up the hallway. I assumed it was Trina due to how slowly the person was moving. I reached in the refrigerator to grab me something to drink just as she walked into the kitchen.

"Why are you screaming so loud?" she asked, sounding out of breath and holding her side. I looked at her, and even though a few days had passed since the fight between her and Ronnie, you could tell who came out on top in the fight, and it wasn't Trina.

"And why are you walking through my house acting as though you own everything?"

"Because I do," I said, shrugging my shoulders as I lifted the drink to my lips, taking a long satisfying drink of my soda.

"Ahhh, that hit the spot."

"What the fuck are you doing here, Michael? I don't have time for your bullshit today. I am in a lot of pain, and frankly, I'm sick of your indecisive, uncaring ass being in my face, so what the fuck do you want?"

"First of all, you can pipe down with that disrespectful ass tone. I came by to check on you and my son. I just wanted to make sure you're OK and don't need anything," I said, pulling her to me and trying to kiss her on the lips, but she turned her head, and my lips landed on her ear. She started with this soft cackle but then it got out of control, like what I said was a joke that had a punch line only she got.

"Our son? Is that what you said? Our son? You see, before I light into that ass, I want to make sure I heard you correctly, because if I'm hearing you clearly, you specifically said our son."

I sucked my teeth and rubbed my hand down my face in total frustration because I sure as hell didn't come here to argue. I came here to get her help, and I had to get her to calm down.

"Yes, our son. You have a problem with me saying that?"

"No the fuck I don't, but what I do have a problem with is you claiming my son when it is convenient for you. Today he's ours, and tomorrow he's mine. And depending on the situation with your wife, he's just mine. I can't with this back and forth. He doesn't deserve it. Because of our fuck up, he's here, and you need to get your shit together because I am done hiding him in the shadows."

I looked at her, knowing that I could never publicly claim him, and I contemplated letting Jay-D's lil' friend just take them out which would solve a lot of my problems, but I couldn't chance her taking out Veronica. I still needed her for now.

"Look, you're right. I have to be better with both of you, and I promise to try to be better for both of you, okay?" I said, looking into her eyes with as much sincerity as possible.

"I can't keep putting him through this, and I sure as hell *won't* keep putting up with it. I will go to court and fuck up everything if you keep picking her over us. Promise that, moving forward, we come first?"

"Of course," I said, knowing good and hell well as soon as

I could get rid of her and the son she wanted me to claim in front of everyone, I was taking that opportunity. I pulled her to me and kissed her deeply. When she reciprocated, I knew I had her right where I wanted her. Our kisses became hungrier and hungrier until she winced in pain.

"Oh, I'm sorry. You're still in pain. Why don't I take care of you tonight?"

She smiled as I led her to the bedroom by the hand. I led her to the bed, and she sat down.

"Scoot back," I commanded as squatted I down between her legs. She winced in pain as she scooted back on the bed, but that didn't faze me. My concern was giving her so much pleasure that I was back in her good graces, and she would fall in line for what I had in store for Mr. Jay-D.

I pulled the gown she was wearing up to her waist and started planting slow deliberate kisses on the inside of her thighs. She started squirming from the slightest skin-to-skin contact I gave her. I kissed my way up to the area between her joint and her pussy, and her breathing increased just from the anticipation of me placing my mouth on her pussy. With the back of my forefinger, I slowly and lightly touched her clit, and she lifted her hips, trying to get me to apply more pressure, but I pulled my hand back which drove her crazy.

"Baby, please. I need to be fucked so bad," she said, begging in a soft and sultry voice.

"Nah. What's all that shit you were talking five minutes

ago?" I asked, blowing on her pussy through the thin panties she was wearing.

"Oh my gosh! Fuck me."

I grabbed the corners of her panties, and she lifted her ass up as I slid them down her legs and threw them on the floor next to me. I stared at the glistening mound before me as she tried to move her hand between her legs to play with her pussy. I slapped her hand away and started blowing on her clit, adding slow, deliberate kisses on her lips, causing her pussy to leak more of her juices that I loved.

"Mmmm, that feels so good!" she said in a breathy tone. I took the tip of my tongue and flicked it across her clit, inserting my middle finger slowly in and out of her pussy. She started bucking her hips, trying to get me to go deeper and apply more pressure to her clit, and every time she did, I stopped.

"Please don't stop. It feels so good," she moaned. I smirked as I grabbed her ass and pulled her pussy closer to my face, dipping my tongue so deep in her pussy that her walls gripped it, and I couldn't pull out.

"Oh fuck, I'm cumming." she said softly.

When her body stopped convulsing, I lifted my head up and looked at her, and she was so spent she was starting to fall asleep. I went to the bathroom and brushed my teeth and washed my face. I grabbed a rag off the shelf in her bathroom and wet it with warm water and soap so I could clean her up. When I finished cleaning her up, I pulled the cover over her, kissed her on the lips, and tried to quietly leave the bedroom, when she called my name with a look of pleasure all over her.

"What did you come over to talk to me about?" I smirked as I walked out of the room, giving her my answer.

"Nothing. We'll talk about it tomorrow. I love you," I added for good measure. It was at that moment I knew, no matter what, Trina would be in on my plan, no matter the cost. If only she knew my plan included getting my wife back and getting rid of Jay-D to save my ass. At this point, she could get on board and play her role or be a casualty in what was to come. Either way, I was going to get what I wanted. I left her house knowing my plan was going to soon be in full effect.

I SAT in a booth in the rear of the restaurant, waiting for the mystery woman to arrive, and I was nervous as hell. I kept checking over my shoulder to see if anyone else was paying attention to me, but I didn't notice anything out of the ordinary. I turned around, and there she was sitting right before me.

"What the fuck! What were you raised by, ninjas or something?"

"Why so jumpy, Mr. Boudreaux? Is there something you're not telling me?"

"No. It's just that you and your people are a little intimidating." She let out a soft chuckle.

"That they are. Now how do you plan to get me my money back?"

"OK, here's the deal. The new owner, Jay-D, is screwing my wife, which is why the money is missing. She left me and took the money in our account because she thought it was money her father had given her. The only way I can get it back is if she and I get back together, which is where you come in." She sat staring at me with a blank expression on her face until a lone tear started running down her cheek.

"Is this a fucking joke? Are you trying to play me? Did Jayson send you?" She sat looking at me with confusion and anger written all over her face.

"What the fuck are you talking about? You called me, remember? And how do you know Jay-D?'

"We used to date until he found out I was sleeping with my father's right hand. I got drunk one night, and he took advantage of me and constantly threatened to tell Jayson if I stopped sleeping with him. Jayson's the only man I ever loved and the only man I will ever love. If you can figure out a way to get us back together, I'm all in. I'll even pay off your debt to my father, assuming it's good." I looked at her with a sheepish grin and got to laying the groundwork for my plan to trap Jay-D in a compromising position with ol' girl.

After laying out the plan, we set up a time to meet, and we figured the office would be the perfect place to do so. I knew Veronica was going to be so easy to manipulate since her trust was so fragile right now. One small misstep and she was gone, and our years together would make me the best candidate to pick up the broken pieces. I smiled as I drove off knowing soon, I would be running the Damien brother's company, and my father-in-law would see that I was ready to run his. Life was going to be even better than it was before the revelation of my affair, as soon as my wife was back where she belonged.

16

JAY-D

I maneuvered my way around my bedroom, trying to avoid all of the boxes that Veronica had yet to unpack. She and I had gotten hot and heavy over the past several months, and I was constantly trying to make a commitment, but she continued to straddle the fence with her decision. She was so worried about what people would think that she was not living or allowing herself to be happy. If she knew what I was doing to her birth control, she would really be pissed.

I loved this girl so much, I googled what candies could be used to replicate birth control and found a company that could make the birth control candy look like actual birth control, and I replaced her birth control with the candy lookalikes. Hell, if I didn't know myself the shit was fake, I would swear they were the real thing.

It had been three months since I did that shit, and her ass hadn't said a damn thing about being pregnant. I knew one thing; if her ass was pregnant and she was making plans without my input, I swear I'd kill her ass.

She walked in the bathroom and kissed me on my cheek before sitting on the toilet to pee. I watched her out of the corner of my eye as she wiped her ass, to make sure she wasn't bleeding and trying to hide it.

"Why are you watching me wipe my ass? That's a little creepy and not seductive at all." I walked out the bathroom without responding to her question and started putting my clothes on.

"What's your problem?" she asked when she came out of the bathroom.

"Nothing. I just have a lot on my mind. Work and the fact that you've still got one foot out the door has me wondering if you'll ever be in a place to commit, that's all." She walked up to me, wrapping her arms around my waist.

"I promise to have everything unpacked by the weekend, okay? Just don't kick me out yet." She looked at me, and I couldn't help but smile at the goofy grin she had plastered on her face that seemed to make her eyes light up. I planted a kiss on her lips and pulled her arms from around my waist so I could finish getting ready.

"Is that it? You have nothing else to say?"

"Look, we have been doing this dance for several months

now, and I feel like you are not all in like I am. I can't force you to have the same feelings for me that I have for you. All I'm asking is that if you don't feel the same way, you tell me, that's all."

"What you think, I'm not all in? After everything I've been through, you think I would put someone else through that same heartache and pain?" She stood looking at me with a look of disbelief and shock, like what I just said hurt her to her core.

"Look," I started as I reached for her arm, and she snatched away. I gave her a stare down that made her come to her senses, and she grabbed my outstretched hand.

"I know you've been through a lot, and I'm not trying to rush you into another situation. I just want to make sure you're all in because leaving isn't an option."

"I know. I'm ready, and I promise I'll have everything unpacked by the time you get home, okay?" I kissed her on the lips and smacked her on the ass and grabbed my stuff so I could head out for work. As I got in my car, my phone rang. I looked at the caller ID and saw it was the office, so I didn't answer because I felt whatever it was, it could wait until I got there. If it was an emergency, Margie would call back. As I pushed the button to start my car, my cell phone started ringing again, and I waited for the car to start up so the Bluetooth would pick up before I answered it. I knew it was something going on because Margie didn't call me back to back unless it was a real emergency.

"Good morning, Ms. Margie. What's going on? Everything okay?"

"Well that depends. You told me to call you if that scoundrel Michael showed up here acting strange; well that's what I'm calling about." I chuckled into the phone because Ms. Margie was a sweetheart and got along with everybody it seemed but Michael.

"Okay. I'm headed that way now, so I should be there soon."

"Well, there is one other thing."

"Well what is it?" I said into the phone a little louder than I intended to. I loved Ms. Margie, but she could be a bit melodramatic when she wanted to be.

"He showed up here with some strange Spanish speaking woman who walked up in here like she owned the place. When I tried to make her sit in the waiting room, she barged right by me, and that snake was right behind her with a smirk on his face. If I had my way, I would have smacked that silly grin right off of his stupid face," she said, ranting.

"Ms. Margie, Ms. Margie!" I yelled, getting her attention. "I'll be there in a few." I hung up the phone, speeding to my office, wondering who this anonymous Spanish speaking woman could be. As I began to ponder who it could be, one person popped in my head, but I knew it couldn't be her stupid ass. I told her crazy ass that we were through, so I didn't know why she felt that it was fucking necessary for her to keep intruding on my fucking life.

I got to my office in record time and stormed into the office without speaking to anyone, because I was on a mission, and if the person I thought was here, was sitting in my office, I was going to choke the shit out of her ass. I walked to my office and stood in the doorway, and she had her ass sitting in my chair while Michael sat off to the side with a stupid smirk on his face.

"What the fuck are you doing here?" I asked her through clenched teeth, still standing in the doorway with my hands balled in a fist, ready to knock the shit out of her if she got my time wrong. She got up and walked toward me in a seductive manner, and I wasn't gon' lie; my dick had a reaction, but it was not because I wanted her. It was simply from familiarity.

"Hola, Papi."

"Get rid of that Spanish accent shit. You and I both know you are from South Florida, so again, I ask you, what... the... fuck... are... you... doing... here?" I asked, drawling each word out slow and deliberately.

"I told you I wouldn't let you go, but you didn't believe me," she said, dropping the Spanish accent.

"Whoa, your ass isn't Spanish?" Michael's dumb ass jumped out of his chair and stalked toward her like he was going to hit her.

"Aye yo, fuck boy, I told yo' ass about trying to hit a female in my presence. You ain't gonna do shit. Matter of fact, you can get the fuck out of my office," I said, not taking my eyes off of Leilani.

"Nah, I'm good," this bitch nigga said and proceeded to walk back to the chair he was sitting in and sit down.

"Leave us," Leilani commanded when she saw me looking at Michael with my fists balled up and my jaw clenched so tight you could see the muscles in my jaw tense up and hear my teeth grinding. Michael looked like he wanted to protest against her request, but when Leilani shot him a dirty look, he thought again and got his snake ass out of my office. He exited my office and sat in the waiting room on. I could see him sulking through the glass wall separating my office from the waiting room. Right now the wall was clear. When I wanted privacy I could frost it which allowed me to see out but no one could see in. I turned my attention back to her, trying to figure out why the hell she was here.

"What the fuck do you want, Leilani? I thought I made myself clear the last time you showed up unannounced."

"You've changed. There's something different about you. You seem... happy," she said, completely ignoring the question I'd just asked her.

"Have you met someone," she asked. I stood watching her stare out of the office window, waiting for a response.

"Who I am or am not with is none of your fucking business, so again, I ask why the fuck are you here?"

"I thought if I gave you time to come to your senses, you would find your way back to me. That if I was just patient and waited, you would realize that I'm the only one for you," she said, walking over to me, getting just close enough that the smell of her perfume made its way up to my nose, bringing up memories of what once was. She saw the faraway look in my eyes and began to run her hand down the side of my face and down the length of my body. I grabbed her hand just as she made her way down to my manhood. I threw her hand away from me and leaned over to her ear so she could get every word I was saying.

"You *were* the only one for me until you fucked that up by fucking another man. Now take your minion and get the fuck out of my office." She looked at me with shock all over her face before a sinister smile began to spread across hers.

"What would my father think of the man who broke his little girl's heart, huh? Dropped her and made her abort his child by threatening her very existence. I wonder what he would say to that," she said, cocking her head to the side with a blank expression on her face. Leilani's father was a ruthless, no nonsense man who ran drugs for the cartel for all of South Florida. If you lived in Florida and had any dealings in the drug industry, you at some point would come in contact with her father. If anyone knew him, they knew he loved two things: making money and his spoiled and only daughter, Leilani.

When we first broke up, I caught hell from him because I allowed her to place the blame on me to save face. I had enough going on with the situation with these gotdamn brothers. I didn't have time to be battling with her father as well, but I wasn't no punk either. I walked up to her as close as I could and stared into her eyes.

"Are you threatening me? Because you of all people know I don't give a fuck who your father is. I fear no man. I wonder what he would think about his daughter fucking his number two man?"

"Well it would be your word against mine. No one told you about Pedro's unfortunate accident? Tsk, tsk, tsk. He really should have been careful where he stored the fuel for his race cars. I hear the gas can be very explosive."

Her laugh was what one would expect to hear from a serial killer or psychopath. She looked at me, face all serious.

"Did you know who the Damien brothers were paying? No?" she asked with a look on her face like she knew something I didn't, but she was itching to share because I had a feeling it would have a huge impact on my life and business, and somehow she would benefit from my situation.

"Well let me enlighten you. The Damien brothers were trying to sell this business to get from under my father's thumb. You see, all of the gambling and drugs they were purchasing to entertain potential clients, left them in the red. They were paying him back by letting him invest in their business, but who would have thought a smart and shrewd businessman would purchase the business right from under them. My father was impressed by the way."

"I'm still waiting for you to tell me what the fuck any of this has to do with me."

"Well they skipped town without paying my father, and their sudden demise makes it impossible for them to pay him back, so the way he sees it, you should have done your research and made sure that the money that was owed him was paid in full. So now, you owe him. You can either pay him the money he's owed in full or do business with him. Either way, he wants his money back." I didn't let this bitch see me sweat because I knew that was why she was here, and the way she ended her last statement, I knew there was another offer.

"Well seeing as how I have daddy wrapped around my finger, I can get him to reconsider the debt for say us getting back together and starting over with a new slate. I mean, think of the benefits of our reunion. Besides, you wouldn't want anything to happen to your precious Veronica, now would you?" Her statement was both casual and threatening, which I took seriously.

I rushed Leilani so quick even she was confused. I had her pinned to the wall by her throat, ready to take my chances with her father, and choke the life out of this crazy bitch. The strange part was she didn't scream or cry. After her initial confusion, this bitch actually started playing with her pussy.

"Mmmm, I love it when you get rough, papi. You have no idea how bad I want to fuck you right now." She lifted her dress, revealing the fact that she had no panties on. I dropped her and walked back to my desk, putting an adequate amount of space between me and her. I had a lot of self-control, but next to Baby Girl, Leilani's pussy always was a weak spot for me. It wasn't that I was in love with her, but shit, I was a man.

"Get the fuck out of my office and stay the fuck away from my girl, or I swear I'll take my chances with your father and slit your fuckin' throat."

"Don't threaten me with a good time," she said, pulling a compact out of her purse and applying more lipstick before grabbing her things and walking out of my office. She stopped in the doorway with the door open and her hand on the doorknob and turned to look back at me before making me aware of her father's deadline.

"This offer won't last forever. You have forty-eight hours before my father collects, so be smart." She blew me a kiss and walked out the door. Her lil' flunky, who had been waiting for her in the waiting room, fell into step right behind her. I slammed the door shut behind her and sat down so hard in my seat, I almost toppled over. I was pissed that I had let my guard down with such a crazy ass woman. When me and Leilani were dating, she was never this desperate. She was always needy but never desperate.

"Argh!" I yelled, frustrated. I had to figure out how to handle this shit and fast, because I wasn't giving up my girl for nobody.

I picked up the phone and called Tech because I needed him to figure out a way to get out of this shit and find out how he missed those fuck ass Damien brothers being in business with Leilani's father.

"We need to fucking talk," I said without even a hello.

"Well hello to gotdamn you too. What the fuck is yo' problem, and why are you making it mine?"

"Well I hired yo' ass to handle all things technical, meaning finding any and all paperwork pertaining to businesses I purchase, including business with hidden contracts and clauses. So how in the fuck did it escape you that them fuck ass Damien brothers were in business with the biggest damn supplier of dope in the south?"

"What the fuck are you talking about? I did research on the company, and nothing came up except the unexplained transactions from the offshore accounts. Other than that, nothing."

"Do me a favor and keep looking into those accounts, because I have a feeling that whatever the brothers and Michael were into had something to do with those accounts. And Tech, don't make me wait."

"I got you. I'll get on that and try to have some answers for you by the end of the week." We hung up the phone without another word, and I continued to contemplate how the fuck I got into this mess.

Leilani and I had a tumultuous past. I was in the streets hard at that time, with all of my focus being on revenge. I was man enough to admit I neglected her needs, and while I was never unfaithful to her, she was, and that ended us. I even allowed her to save face and tell her father it was me, and now that shit was coming back to bite me in the ass. I had to figure out a way to fix this shit so it didn't affect Baby Girl. She'd been hurt enough, and my bullshit couldn't be the reason she ended up hurt again.

I grabbed my jacket and left the office to clear my head. I had to come up with a plan and quick because the last thing I wanted was to lose the best thing that walked into my life over an ex who meant absolutely nothing to me.

17

VERONICA

I sat on the toilet staring at two blue lines, and I almost fainted. I hadn't been feeling well, but not like a flu or cold sick, but how I felt when I was pregnant. I sat thinking to myself how the fuck I was so careless and let this happen. I sat here running the couple of months back in my head and I couldn't recall missing my pill once. I mean I was questioning my own sanity and the efficacy of birth control at this point. I mean the only thing I could think of was that time I was on antibiotics, but that was right after my last miscarriage so I know that couldn't be it. Everything that has gone on in my life as of recent, makes me question whether or not I'm ready or even want to have another baby. I checked my birth control packages to see if my pills were off, like maybe I missed some days, and the pills that were supposed to be missing were missing so I don't understand what happened.

The only thing that was missing was the doctor label with my doctor's name. I looked closer and noticed something off with the package. I went to grab the new refill I had just picked up and noticed that the two packages were different. For one, the label on the one I had been taking had the wrong doctor's name on it. I figured maybe there was a mix-up, but my name was on the packet but the name and dosage of the medicine matched. Upon closer inspection, I noticed the pills were completely different. You didn't notice unless you were looking for it, but there was a difference. I picked up my phone and started calling Jayson and accidentally answered a call coming through. I checked my caller ID and it was Trina. I knew I should have blocked this bitch. I just held the phone to my ear because I felt if this bitch was calling me, she must have something to say.

"Hello!" She said with hesitation.

"Ronnie, are you there?" She asked in a soft voice.

"Yeah, and out of all the people I answered the phone for, it had to be you. I don't know why the fuck you're calling, but make what you have to say quick I have a call to make. I don't know what a simple bitch who fucked my husband, pretended to be my friend, and allowed me to be godparent of a child I'm actually the stepparent for, has to say to me. This is going to be interesting." I said, letting out a laugh so maniacal I scared myself.

"You want an apology, fine I'm sorry for not being honest sooner, I'm sorry for not letting you know of our relationship sooner, and allowing you to waste your time on a man who meant you no good, but what I will not apologize for is what led to me having my son. And the way I see it after that dinner we had, we're even." I pulled the phone away from my ear and stared at it like this bitch was sitting in my face.

"How...in...the...fuck did you come to that conclusion?" I asked her, enunciating every word slowly and deliberately.

"The way I see it, you took what was mine, and I just returned the favor but on a grander scale." This bitch had lost her mind if she thought what she did at any point and time was anywhere near the pain she had put me through.

"You know what keep your fuckin apology because at this point you and Michael mean absolutely nothing to me. It's partially my fault anyway, because I was warned when we were in high school that you were a selfish, conniving, and inconsiderate bitch, but me being who I am I just had to take in a stray. Had I not tried to be captain save-a-hoe, and actually listened, you would still be a two-dollar ho sucking and fucking everything with a dick for clout. Hell, you sure Michael is even your son's father?" She let out a sinister laugh.

"Well one thing about it, Michael saw this as his only chance to have a child and signed the birth certificate. You know of any other kids he may have out there, cause I sure as hell don't, so fuck you, you barren bougie bitch." *Beep. Beep.* I checked my phone and this tramp had hung up on me. I was pissed I had let that THOT get to me. Here I am, attempting to move on with my life and this bitch is on my line with a fake ass apology. I have enough going on right now, and I don't need the extra drama. Which led me back to why I had my phone in my hand. I dialed his number and got no answer. I sent him a text, letting him know we needed to talk so he needed to call me. I finished up in the bathroom and headed downstairs and started getting everything out to prepare dinner. I loved cooking, especially when I had a lot on my mind. I was pissed at Jayson for pulling the shit he did with regards to my pills, but wondered if this was a blessing in disguise. My emotions were all mixed up. I got everything I would need for our dinner and started preparing my meal. As I began seasoning and prepping, my mind drifted to where I was now, a married woman about to have a baby with another man. I'm pissed about the fact he did some sneaky shit instead of talking to me about what he wanted from me. I mean that was below underhanded and sneaky. I haven't even figured out my life right now let alone bringing a child into this confusing and crazy situation that I don't know if I'm even ready for.

"God what do I do?" It was at that moment, I remembered that I'm still married to Michael, and if or when I have this child it would be his by law.

"Fuck! I have got to divorce Michael before he finds out about this pregnancy." If he finds out about this baby, I'll be creating a mountain of problems that I don't really need at this moment. I had been in the kitchen putting the finishing touches on dinner when my phone dinged. I looked at the time and figured it was Jayson finally returning my text from earlier. I wiped my hands on my apron and grabbed my phone to unlock it and check the messages because several had come back to back. When I looked at the screen it was images sent from a number that wasn't saved in my phone and I wasn't familiar with. I opened up the images and I almost dropped my phone. It was pictures of Jayson and some woman I had never seen before, but they seemed quite intimate. He had her against the wall and she had her dressed pulled up with a look of ecstasy on her face. I turned off the stove and sat in one of the chairs at the dining room table unable to move, completely in shock and confused at what I had just seen. Once again, I found myself in the same situation I was in with my husband, and I was not going to end up looking like a fool once again. I sat there and the longer I sat the more pissed I became, I went upstairs and started throwing all of my shit in a bag. If he thought, he was going to play me like Michael, he had another think coming. I picked up the phone and dialed Jayson's number because this time I wasn't going to roll over so easy. The phone rang once and went to voicemail, after calling back to back several times he finally picked up.

"What the fuck do you want, if I'm not answering that means I need a minute, damn what is wrong with women," he said under his breath but I heard him clear as day. I was at that moment I had made my decision about what I was going to do and one of those decisions included not telling him about the baby.

"Are you serious right now? I called you earlier and got no response so I text you that we needed to talk, and trust the only reason I text you was because there was something pressing that we needed to discuss, and now you act like me blowing up your phone is a common occurrence. Since you've known me, have I ever gone out of my way to reach you like this?" I said, raising my voice because at this point, I was heated.

"What cat got your tongue you can't answer?" I said because he wasn't responding to my question quick enough.

"No." He mumbled.

"Then common fucking sense would tell you that either something was wrong or something was really urgent."

"I'm sorry. I have just had a long day; can we please start over?" He asked in a calmer tone, but at this point I was pissed the fuck off and done with him.

"You know what, Jayson, I wish it were that simple. You are not the only one to have a bad day today and starting over is not an option. I swore to myself after Michael I would no longer allow a man to make a fool out of me so I'm done."

"What the fuck are you talking about done? You're done over a simple little argument or a failure to answer a phone call or text. Is it that easy for you to walk away from something I thought we were beginning to build?' He shot off question after question without a break.

"I wish it were as simple as a missed text or phone call." I sent him the texts I received from the unknown number and, I heard multiple beeps on his phone notifying him that he had received text messages.

"What the fuck!" I heard him say.

"Baby Girl, this is not what it looks like. I can explain."

"Jayson, I'm really not interested in an explanation. I've been through enough drama, and I'm not looking for more. I gotta go, and I'll leave your keys on the bar. Goodbye." I said, hanging up the phone. I heard yelling for me to wait as I hung up, but I knew if I stayed on the line, he would somehow change my mind. I called an Uber to pick me up because I didn't want to be here when he arrived. We had been on such a whirlwind with our relationship, I hadn't gotten the chance to pick up my car from the house so I just used one of his, but I was regretting that decision now. After about fifteen minutes, I was done packing and headed out the door because I got a notification that my Uber driver had arrived. I had never packed so fast in my life; I was running around the house like Celie in *The Color Purple* trying to get away from Mister. I did one final swoop of the house and placed Jayson's keys on the bar, locking up after myself. I climbed in the car and laid my head back on the headrest as the driver took off. I looked down at my nonexistent belly and rubbed it as I talked.

"Here on out, kid, it looks like it's just you and me. I have no idea what is going to happen at this point, but I know this area holds too many bad memories, and I need a fresh start. I make you this promise, no matter what happens, and no matter how you came about, I love you already and from here on out we'll weather any storm together." I laid my head back and enjoyed the ride to the airport. I didn't have a plan and had no idea where I was going, but I knew no matter what happened from here on out, I was going to be in charge of my destiny.

18

MICHAEL

I watched and smiled to myself as Ronnie exited the home she was now sharing with Jay-D. She looked pissed which gave me so much pleasure. Since leaving me, she completely ignored my calls and texts, even going as far as to block me from her phone. Hell, to be honest if anyone should be mad it should be Trina, I was with her first. I looked over at Leilani and she had this malicious grin on her face. I wondered what the fuck had her ass so captivated by Jay-D's ass. She sat there watching Ronnie exit Jay-D's apartment and had this grin on her face like the Joker. This woman was bat shit crazy and delusional. She had somehow convinced herself that Jay-D was in love with her ass even lying to Jay-D that her father had beef with him, hell if I do say so myself that last idea was pure genius.

"What now?" I asked. She let out a sinister laugh and as

quickly as she started it was over. Yo, this bitch was crazy for real.

"We've only just begun," she turned to look at me with a serious face.

"Do you honestly think she is out of his system that quick? This is only phase one of my plan. Watch and learn." She said as she started the car and pulled off from the curb. It is so funny how that heavy Spanish accent disappeared after we left Jay-D's office.

"You still didn't answer my question, what do we do now?"

"How the fuck you pull off being with two women for years is beyond me, because it's clear you have no fucking clue how to plan anything." She pulled up to my car and I stared at her waiting for a response to my question.

"Ugh, be prepared to answer your phone when you see my number. I don't care if you're in pussy so deep I feel your nut. Answer my call." She said and pulled off barely giving me a chance to get out of her car.

"I hate that bitch." I said under my breath as I watched the back of her car disappear into traffic. I walked over to my car and pulled out my phone to call Trina, and the phone went straight to voicemail. I stared at the phone thinking I had the wrong number, so I ended the call, and tried calling her again and got the voicemail again. I had been so busy dealing with this shit with Leilani, I hadn't had time to check in with Trina. The last time she and I spoke, I tried to get her on board with helping us sabotage Jay-D and Ronnie, but she wanted no parts of it. My influence over her had been waning recently, and I feared that she was completely over me.

"I know this bitch did not change her number on me." I climbed in my car and headed in the direction of the house I paid for. All types of the thoughts were running through my head and one of them being Trina laid up with another nigga. I swear if I got there and that's what was going on, I was putting her, her mammy, and bastard son out tonight. That would be all the proof I needed that she was a whore and her son wasn't mine. I pulled up to the house, and it was dark as fuck.

"Her car must be in the garage." I said to no one in particular. I got out and went to knock on the door and it pushed open.

"What the fuck! Trina!" I yelled, and I got nothing but silence. The house was completely dark and eerie, and the only sound you could hear was the hum of the refrigerator. The icemaker made a loud noise when the ice dropped in the bucket, and I damn near jumped out of my skin. The closer I got to Trina's bedroom, the more eerie it seemed things got. When I finally got to her room, the door was ajar, and I saw a lump laying on the bed. I called Trina's name and got no answer, so I walked over to where the lump was and nudged it with my hand and heard a soft, raspy moan. I went to turn on the lights and the bulb was taken out. I turned the flashlight on, on my phone and what was before me scared the fuck out of me. Trina's face was all distorted from what seemed like a gunshot wound. She couldn't have been laying here like this long because the blood on her face and surrounding area was still wet. I immediately called 9-1-1 and ran to my son's room to check on him. All I could do was pray as I walked down the hallway. For all the shit I talked and all the bullshit I said to his mama, I didn't want anything to happen to my son. I slowly pushed the door open and saw the television light shining, and the shadow of a figure sitting in the gaming chair we got for his last birthday. I walked around and caught sight of my son and dropped to my knees. My son was slumped over in his chair with the game controller in his hand like he never saw whatever it was coming. Whoever it was must have snuck up behind him and shot him in the head. I reached over and checked for a pulse and got nothing. His body was still warm, so I know he couldn't have been here like this for long. I heard this gut wrenching, soul piercing scream and when I looked up, police came rushing into the room, and I realized it was me that was screaming. I exited the room to head back to where Trina was, while the paramedics walked passed me and headed into my son's room to attempt to help him, but I knew it was futile, he was already gone. I looked down at the bloody figure on the bed and tried to gain my composure, because I knew this was going to kill her. Trina kept trying to say something, but I couldn't understand her because her mouth was all distorted from the gunshot wound. Whoever shot her must have thought she was dead because of how much blood was in the room. There was another set of paramedics trying to work on her, but she kept trying to fight them. I don't know where she found the strength, because she looked like she was knocking at death's door. As the paramedics past me with her on the stretcher, she signaled for them to stop in front of me. She kept whispering something, so I leaned in closer so I could hear what she was saying.

"Jamon?" she asked in a soft, but questioning tone. I tried to avoid answering, but the look on my face must have told her wanted she wanted to know, and if that didn't confirm it the stupid ass detective did.

"Whoever came in here and did this was a sick fuck for what they did to that boy." Trina looked back and forth between me and the detective, and when I didn't clarify his statement, she knew what had happened.

"Noooooo!" Trina just started wailing. Everyone looked at the detective like they wanted to shoot him right between the eyes. His appearance was that of someone who was just riding the wave until he could retire, letting everyone in the house at that time know he no longer gave a fuck. I started stomping toward him, eyes locked on him, as if he was the prey and I was the predator, he began to busy himself as though not looking at me could erase the damage he just caused. I felt a firm hand on my chest, stopping me from getting my hands on him, and I looked down at the hand of the person who was about to take their last breath. When my eyes finally made contact with the person in my path, a calm washed over me. I met a pair of the sweetest, kindest deep set, dark brown eyes that looked like they were seeing into my very soul. At that moment, my murder mission was put on pause while I took in the beauty that was standing before me. Now while this woman was attractive with her chocolate skin, and a smile that would make even the hardest day seem easy, it wasn't about that for me at this time. It was like she was surrounded by a cloud of calm energy, and I got swept in with her. My trance was broken when the other paramedic that was with her called her to assist her with getting Trina on the ambulance because he couldn't handle her in her distraught state. She kept trying to get off of the stretcher, so they had to secure her legs and arms to the bed to keep her from falling and hitting the concrete ground. Once they got her secure, the beautiful paramedic looked back at me to see if I wanted to ride, and I said no. I would meet them back at the hospital once I finished up here. I headed back in the house and before I could enter the doorway good, I heard a loud, zipping noise. At that moment, time stood still and the only thing I could think was everything I said and everything I did with regards to my son; I wish I could take back. I always felt I had time to make everything up to him, and that when he got older, he would understand why I had to do things, regarding him and his mother, the way I did. Now, there was no making it right, there was no when he got older.

He would always be stuck in my heart and mind as a child. I would never give him advice for his first date, or watch him grow into the amazing man I knew he could be. My heart hurt more than I could ever explain. I finished talking to the cops and giving them everything I could, which was nothing, and hopped in my car to head to the hospital to check on Trina. When I arrived at the hospital, I walked up to the front desk to give my information, but because she was a shooting victim and I wasn't her husband, they wouldn't let me up. I sat downstairs in the waiting room with the hopes that I could figure out a way to sneak upstairs to see her. I was sitting there for about fifteen minutes when one of the security guards walked outside for what looked like a smoke break. I waited a minute then followed him outside to see if he would sneak me upstairs.

"Yo, my man, let me holla at you for a minute." He looked me up and down like I had shit all over my face.

"What?"

"Listen, my girl is upstairs, and I need to check on her. I'll give you a stack if you can get me up there." He turned his back as though our conversation was over so I started back inside when I heard him clear his throat.

"Cash App me the money and meet me in the cafeteria." He gave me his Cash App name, and I prayed that the amount in there would cover it, and when I saw that green check mark, I knew we were good. I waited for him in the cafeteria for what seemed like forever, when he showed up to take me to the elevators. He gave me the information to get to Trina's room and when I arrived on the ICU floor where she was, it was quiet. As I walked up to the door to get buzzed in, her mother was coming out, and the look on her face let me know she was about to come with the bullshit. She walked up to me and slapped me so hard I almost forgot she was a woman and hit her back.

"You get away from this hospital and don't you dare come back. I don't know how, but I know whatever happened here is your fault. My daughter is fighting for her life and my grandson is dead because of you so GET OUT, GET OUT, GET OUT!" She screamed, making everyone in the area near us stop and stare in our direction. I attempted to explain but she put her hand up to stop me before I could get a single word out.

"I don't know who did this but I know it had something to do with you and whatever you have had your hands in so let my daughter grieve in peace and stay the fuck away. Please." She said almost begging. I stood there for a moment contemplating my next move but figured it was best if I just left now and waited until Trina was able to tell me herself that she wanted me to stay away. As I walked back to my car, I became enraged and wondered who in the fuck could do something so callous. My mind wandered to Leilani, and I felt like her family was the only one ruthless enough to carry out a hit like this. I pulled out my phone and shot her a text message, telling her we needed to talk. I arrived at my car and pulled out my keys to unlock the door when I felt something sharp stick me in my neck. I hadn't been paying attention to my surroundings but when I looked up, I saw the reflection of a figure in the driver's side window, standing next to me in a dark hoodie and a face mask covering their face, when all of a sudden everything started fading to black. All I could think to myself before the darkness took over was that I was going to be able to see my son again, and a smile spread across my face until my mind was clear.

19

JAY-D

I rushed home as fast as I could because I didn't want Baby Girl to leave before I could explain the pictures. I don't know how I allowed myself to get caught in such a compromising position. I knew Leilani's sneaky ass was up to something when she chose to show up with that snake ass Michael.

"Fuck!" I yelled, hitting the steering wheel because I was getting frustrated at the slow-moving traffic. I kept changing lanes and cutting people off all the while praying that I made it home in time to stop her from making a decision I know in the long run she would regret. Hell, I didn't even know if she was pregnant with my kid.

"Man, I've got to get home." I pressed the gas harder going ninety miles per hour and praying that I wouldn't get pulled over. Twenty minutes later, I was pulling into my driveway not caring how I parked because I was in such a hurry. I jumped out of the car, leaving it running with the key in the ignition and the door wide open. I looked over and saw all of the cars in the driveway which gave me a glimmer of hope that she was still here. I used the code to unlock the door, and I burst into the house calling Baby Girl's name.

"Veronica!" I shouted as I sprinted upstairs, leaving the front door open and going from room to room checking for her.

"Veronica!" I called again, getting no answer. When I got to the master bedroom, I let out a sigh of relief because nothing seemed out of place, however, my stomach dropped when I entered her walk-in closet and saw the drawers pulled out and sitting empty. I still held out hope thinking maybe she was in a hurry to get out that she just took what was in the dresser. When I opened the closet doors where she hung her clothes, and there was nothing there but hangers, I knew she was gone. I slid down the wall with my face in my hand upset that it seemed like I had just missed her.

"Argh!" I got up and knocked all of the hangers down to the floor that were hanging in what used to be Baby Girl's closet. I slowly dragged myself downstairs to see if it was possible that she left a note or anything to tell me where she could possibly be. I tried calling her phone as I walked downstairs to check the kitchen for a possible note. My calls kept going to voicemail which meant she either had her phone turned off or she had me blocked, either way I was growing more and more frustrated with each passing moment. I wish at this time I had her father's number because other than Michael I didn't know anyone else that was a part of her life. I sat in the bar stool praying that this was a nightmare and that I would wake up soon, but nothing. I sat at the bar with my head sitting in my hands realizing this woman jumped to conclusions without giving me a chance to explain. She automatically assumed I was screwing someone else without even hearing my side. Hell, if that was how it would be loving her than fuck her, I don't need her in my life. All of a sudden, I felt a presence behind me, thinking it was Baby Girl. I swiftly turned around and saw a dark figure standing behind me before everything went dark.

Several hours later and I was waking up in a dark room. I was groggy and my head hurt like I had been dosed with heavy drugs. I tried to sit up but the room would spin, and I felt like I was going to lose whatever food I had left in my stomach right there. My senses slowly started to awaken, and I realized that I must have been in a hotel room somewhere. I slowly started feeling around on the bed and my hand hit what felt like a person in the bed with me, but whoever it was had what felt like a sheet covering their body, and I couldn't see because of how dark the room was. The bed felt wet, and I tried to wipe my hand on my pants but realized at that moment I was naked. Now I was really feeling like something was going on because the last thing I remembered was sitting at the bar in my kitchen trying to figure out where things with Baby Girl went left. I was determined to figure out what the fuck was going on and how the hell I got here. I began stumbling my way around the room for a lamp or light switch so I could see who was lying next to me.

"Shit!" I yelled after I hit my shin on what must have been the corner of the bed. This had to be one of those cheap ass, pay by the hour places because it smelled like cigarettes and mildew in here, and the curtains had the room so dark I couldn't see my hand in front of my face. I finally found a light switch and turned it on. I almost fell over when I saw the sight before me. There was blood everywhere, the walls, the bed, hell even the lamps were covered in blood. It looked like a scene straight out of a horror movie like some *Texas Chainsaw Massacre* type shit. I creeped closer to the body and jumped back when I realized it was Leilani lying there. I put my hands on each side of my head and paced back and forth in the room wondering if anybody saw me come in here, and how the fuck I got in here in the first place. I started looking around the room for my clothes so I could get the fuck out of her and figure out what was going on. I located some pants and a t-shirt in the closet and began to get dressed. As I finished putting the shoes that were two sizes too small on my feet, I heard a loud banging noise on the door. *BAMM, BAMM, BAMM, BAMM!* I heard in rapid succession.

"Police open up!"

"Fuckkk!" I screamed. What is going on. I looked around the room to see if there was another way out like maybe the room had a door leading to the room next to it but nothing. I was turning around in circles when all of the sudden the door to the room was kicked in, and I was tackled by what seemed to be forty officers but was only four. One looked at the bed and looked back at me.

"You sick son of a bitch. Cuff him." He said, looking at me in total disgust. I turned around and placed my hands behind my back. If I learned anything from my time in prison, it's don't say shit. As the cop read me my rights, I said one word, "Attorney."

20

X

I sat in my car watching as Jayson, or Jay-D as he was known in the streets was loaded in the back of the police cruiser with a blank expression on his face. I couldn't tell what he was thinking, but I know he was confused. Especially after finding Leilani in his bed. I picked up the phone to call my boss.

"It's done." I said and hung up the phone. I sat in my car and watched for a minute before slowly pulling away from the curb and driving off. As I passed the police car with Jay-D in the back, I glanced his way to get a closer look. The way he stared at the car as though he could see beyond the dark tint, I'll admit had me a little shook. Out of all the years I've worked for Mr. B we never allowed work to hit close to home. I hope he knew what he was doing because I have a feeling he just opened a can of worms that he won't be able to close.................

To Be Continued

Made in the USA
Monee, IL
21 July 2020

36808602R00105